ROOM
212

ONE TEACHER. ONE ROOM.
ONE DEGREE THAT CHANGED EVERYTHING.

ROOM 212

BRAD JOHNSON

Extended Study Guide
Reflection & Discussion for Each Chapter
© 2025 Brad Johnson
The right of Brad Johnson to be identified as the author of this work
has been asserted in accordance with the U.S. Copyright Act of 1976.

Room 212: The Teacher Who Changed Everything
An EduFable™ by Brad Johnson
ISBN: 979-8-9992052-0-9 (Paperback)
ISBN: 979-8-9992052-1-6 (eBook)
Library of Congress Control Number: 2025912770
Library of Congress Cataloging-in-Publication Data
Names: Johnson, Brad, **1969–**, author.
Title: *Room 212: the teacher who changed everything / Brad Johnson.*
Description: Atlanta, GA: One Degree Press, 2025.
Identifiers: LCCN 2025912770 | ISBN 979-8-9992052-
0-9 (paperback) | ISBN 979-8-9992052-1-6 (ebook)
Subjects: LCSH: Teachers—Conduct of life. | Motivation in education.
Classification: LCC LB1775 .J645 2025 (print) | DDC 371.1—dc23
LC record available at https://lccn.loc.gov/2025912770
First published 2025
by One Degree Press
Atlanta, Georgia
www.OneDegreePress.com
Cover design and interior layout by Damonza
For permissions, bulk orders, or speaking engagements, contact:
info@DoctorBradJohnson.com

CONTENTS

Acknowledgments

Room 212 has been a deeply personal journey, and I'm grateful to those who helped bring it to life.

Thank you to **Laurel Hecker** for your editorial expertise and thoughtful guidance—you helped shape this story into something truly worthy of the teachers it honors.

To the creative team at **Damonza**, your design brought the vision to life with clarity and impact. I'm grateful for your talent and professionalism.

A special thank you to **Jeremy Johnson**, whose early editorial input and content collaboration laid the foundation for this book. Your voice and belief in this project mattered deeply.

And to my mother, **Carolyn Johnson**—your love of storytelling, quiet strength, and belief in people inspired this book's very heart. Thank you for giving me the roots to write it.

This book is for the teachers who show up, day after day—not for recognition, but because they lead with heart.

—Dr. Brad Johnson

THE TRUTH BEHIND ROOM 212

Room 212 is a fable, but it's built on truth.

The classroom moments. The hallway conversations. The exhausted silences and the small but meaningful breakthroughs. Every scene was inspired by real experiences from real schools—drawn from my own journey as a teacher, administrator, and education leader.

Tammy was based on the best teacher I ever taught with. But truthfully? I've known several Tammys.

They were assertive yet compassionate. Calm in the chaos. Steady in the storm. They made learning come alive. They were relatable. They were real. These were the teachers who didn't need a spotlight to lead. They showed up every day for kids no one else could reach—not with perfection, but with presence. They didn't preach. They modeled. And they led in a way that left a mark, whether anyone noticed or not.

Tammys are the backbone of every great school.

We all know them. They may go by different names, but their impact is unmistakable. They carry the culture. They hold the line. And they do it with heart, grace, and quiet conviction.

The students in this story aren't based on just one child—but they're all real. Their names have changed, but their stories haven't. If you've been in a classroom long enough, you've met them, too. Maybe you still teach them.

Room 212 isn't just about a classroom.

It's about the kind of teaching that changes lives—built on connection, belief, and the courage to help students become their best.

So, if you've ever doubted your impact...

If you've ever felt unseen, burned out, or unsure if it's worth it...

I hope this story brings you back to your purpose.

Because the truth is simple:

The teacher makes the difference.

Always has. Always will.

—Dr. Brad Johnson

ROOM 212

EVERY SCHOOL HAS a teacher like the one in Room 212.

You might not notice them right away. They don't chase attention. They command it, not with noise, but with presence.

The moment you step into their classroom, something shifts.

The noise settles. The pressure fades. And for a moment, teaching feels like what it was always meant to be human, hopeful, alive.

This isn't a story about programs or initiatives. It's not a formula or a framework.

It's about a teacher named Tammy.

She wasn't the loudest voice in the building. She didn't need a spotlight. But when she stepped into her classroom, things moved. People noticed. Students leaned in.

She taught in Room 212.

It wasn't just a room number. It was a temperature. A shift. The one-degree difference that separated her from everyone else.

At 211 degrees, water is hot. But at 212 degrees, it boils. Boiling water creates steam. And steam moves things.

That one extra degree? It changes everything.

Sometimes, that one degree was a quiet pause instead of a sharp response.

Sometimes, it was calling a student by name before class even started.

Sometimes, it was staying one more minute after the bell just to listen.

Small moves that shifted everything.

Tammy was that extra degree. She didn't rely on flashy lessons or trendy systems. She relied on presence. Patience. Consistency. She built a space where students felt safe, seen, and capable, sometimes for the first time.

And kids flourished, extending from this foundation of trust.

Room 212 wasn't about charisma or control. It was about connection.

It was about showing up, every day, with quiet strength and unwavering belief, even when students didn't show it back.

There are teachers like Tammy in every school. And every teacher has the potential to be that one degree of difference.

This story isn't just about her, it's about what happens when teaching stops being about delivering standards and starts being about building people.

It's about how one teacher in one classroom can change the trajectory of an entire life.

Because the truth is, most teachers live in Room 211. They work hard. They care. They're present. But they're closer than they think to something more. And that one-degree shift is not about longer hours, better slides, or trendy classroom décor.

It's about showing up with intention.

Choosing connection over control, people over policies, purpose over performance.

I didn't start out in Room 212.

In fact, I didn't even know what it meant until I saw it from across the hall. Until I watched Tammy teach without theatrics. Until I saw how she made broken kids feel whole and reminded adults what teaching is really about.

And slowly, I began to realize: Teaching isn't about control.

It's about trust.

It's not about what you deliver.

It's about what you draw out of them.

That's the root of the word *educate*: *educere*—to lead out. To bring forth what's already inside.

Tammy didn't just teach content.

She helped students discover who they were, and in the process, she helped me do the same.

So, if you've ever stood in your classroom wondering if this is worth it; if you've ever felt like you're trying, but not reaching; if you've ever questioned whether your presence matters—this story is for you.

The difference between showing up and showing up with purpose is just one degree.

I didn't know Tammy yet.

I only knew what I'd heard in the hallways, that Room 212 was different. That students changed in there. That the teacher behind that door did something the rest of us couldn't quite explain.

My name is Mitchell Karns, and I taught across the hall in Room 211. On my first day, I walked into chaos…

… and that chaos was the beginning of something great.

THE
SECOND
CAREER

MITCHELL KARNS HAD always known what came next—until he didn't.

For sixteen years, life had followed a predictable trajectory: mechanical engineering degree, project manager by thirty, regional director by thirty-eight. Numbers. Deadlines. Bonuses. Everything clean, measured, and controlled.

But that Tuesday morning, sitting in a glass-walled conference room surrounded by people more obsessed with profit margins than people, Mitchell realized something he couldn't un-realize:

He was building things that didn't matter.

For all the awards on his wall, the corner office, the respect he'd earned, Mitchell had never felt more disconnected from the purpose he craved. The projects he managed didn't fill him; they simply checked boxes. No meeting, no report, no financial incentive had ever connected with him on a human level.

Six months later, the layoff didn't break him. It freed him.

For the first time in years, Mitchell was no longer tethered to a path that didn't resonate with him. Though leaving his field was his choice, it still felt like a jump into the unknown.

At forty-two, he was starting over as a teacher.

Not because he was desperate, but because he was drawn to something real.

Something that, for once, felt authentic.

That's what led him here—his search for something real.

And now, standing at the entrance to Room 211, he clutched his color-coded binder like a shield, trying to steady his shaking hands.

The entire building was chaos.

Not the controlled chaos he'd known in boardrooms where data swirled in manic circles. This was different.

Raw, unscripted, human noise.

The sound of bodies moving, voices clashing, laughter echoing in an unchoreographed rhythm.

It wasn't the work Mitchell had been trained to do.

His old career had been about precision, about getting things exactly right.

But here, there was no such thing as right.

No perfect formula.

No clean answer.

He stood frozen at the door, unsure what to do.

The mismatched desks.

The whiteboard stained with faded equations.

And the nameplate outside: Mr. Karns.

It didn't even look like his name—like someone else had stepped into this life and he was just watching.

In his old world, everything had a place.

Now, nothing made sense.

He opened the blinds, then closed them.

Moved the desks.

Adjusted the marker tray—anything to outrun the growing dread in his chest.

This wasn't the start he'd envisioned.

He had studied the curriculum, spent weeks preparing, pored over materials, made sure everything was in order.

But faced with thirty-six students about to walk into Room 211, all his carefully crafted plans felt like disillusionment.

How could he control any of this?

How could he teach them if everything around him felt out of his control?

Mitchell's hands shook as he fumbled with the lesson plan.

"Hey! You the new guy?"

The voice snapped him back to reality.

Mitchell turned to see a student standing in the doorway, basketball in hand.

Behind him, others shuffled in, some laughing, some already lost in their own conversations.

"Mr. K, right?" the boy asked.

Mitchell tried to speak, but his throat felt tight.

"Yeah. Mr. K. First day," he managed.

The bell rang.

A tidal wave of noise flooded in.

The laughter.

The shouting.

The buzzing of a hundred different conversations colliding.

Mitchell felt completely lost.

His hands shook as he scrambled to take attendance, eyes darting between the roster and the students, trying to match unfamiliar names to unfamiliar faces.

One girl (Jasmine, quiet, earbuds in) refused to answer to her legal name.

A boy (Marcus, loud and already performing) tossed his backpack across the room, missing the hook.

Another girl (Camila, sketching in the margin of her notebook) didn't look up once.

A few students were already asking questions, not waiting for the lesson to begin.

This wasn't supposed to happen.

Mitchell stood there, sweating.

The lesson plan he'd spent hours prepping?

A faint memory.

His organized world of metrics and meetings was miles away.

He thought he could control the classroom.

That he could manage the students the same way he had managed projects.

The reality in front of him?

Completely unpredictable.

By the end of first period, Mitchell sat at his desk, staring at the clock.

He was caught off guard by the chaos, yes.

But what surprised him even more was the overwhelming sense of powerlessness.

There was no department to manage, no meetings to facilitate, no agenda to push forward.

He had no way of measuring his success. His first day felt like a failure. He wasn't sure if he could do this. He didn't know if he even belonged here.

As he watched the second hand tick, a wave of doubt settled over him. This wasn't just a rough day. This was the start of something so far outside his comfort zone that he wasn't sure if he'd ever feel at home again.

Knock, knock.

"You survived," said a voice from the doorway.

Mitchell looked up.

There she was.

Calm. Centered. Unphased by the surrounding chaos.

She stood with quiet authority, coffee in hand, posture relaxed and unshakable. Her presence wasn't loud, but it filled the doorway like a golden light.

This was the teacher from Room 212.

Not just another colleague. Not just another name on the staff list.

Something about her made the noise fade.

"Tammy. Room 212," she said, her voice steady but warm.

Mitchell stood, his voice betraying his nerves as he hurriedly repeated his unpolished introduction from the beginning of first period. "Mr. K. First day."

She looked him up and down with a practiced eye. "Thought so. You've got the look."

"The look?" Mitchell asked, confused.

"The look," she repeated, smirking. "Like someone who spent a lot of time planning something the kids didn't care about."

Mitchell opened his mouth to defend himself, but the words didn't come. She was right. Tammy wasn't being rude. She was honest.

He responded with a dry laugh. "Thanks for the confidence boost."

"Confidence isn't your problem," she said, her tone light but pointed. "It's connection."

She paused as she turned away from the doorway, offering one final thought.

"If you want to survive this year, Mr. Karns, remember this: They don't need someone who knows it all. They need someone who understands them and cares."

Mitchell stood there as her words hung in the air. She hadn't fixed anything, but somehow, she had given him something to hold on to.

He didn't know it then, but that was his first shift in temperature, the first flicker of heat, slowly nudging Room 211 toward something more.

CHAPTER

2

WELCOME TO
ROOM 211

MITCHELL ARRIVED AT school the next morning before sunrise. The building was still dark, the parking lot lit only by flickering streetlights and the occasional flash of a motion sensor near the back entrance. He sat in his car, engine off, sipping lukewarm gas station coffee and watching the mist roll across the field behind the school. It was quiet. Peaceful. Deceptive.

He wasn't here early to get ahead. He was here because he couldn't sleep.

The first day had gone nothing like he expected. He had always believed that preparation guaranteed success, but the kids hadn't read his outline. They didn't care about bullet points or PowerPoint slides. Deep down, that terrified him. For the first time in a long time, Mitchell had to admit that intelligence wasn't going to save him. *Connection would.* But he didn't know how to build that yet.

Inside, Room 211 was exactly as he left it, desks mostly crooked, a whiteboard still smudged from erased equations, a broken pencil wedged into the heater vent. The paper someone had taped to the door with his name still read *Mr. Kramz.*

He sat at his desk and pulled out his planner. He'd written today's objective in neat block letters: *Students will solve two-step equations using inverse operations.*

But the real objective? *Survive.*

He looked around and thought about everything he hadn't been taught: how to earn trust, how to read a room full of twelve- and thirteen-year-olds, how to reset a class that had already written you off. He thought about quitting. He didn't dare say it out loud, but the thought was there. It lingered like the echo of failure.

He looked up at the clock. The same one hung in every corporate boardroom he used to sit in. But time felt different here—slower, less forgiving.

By 7:45, the hallways began to buzz. He could hear the stampede of footsteps, the locker slams, someone laughing too loudly. Then came the bell.

And the door opened.

Jasmine was the first in. She wore oversized headphones and a hoodie with the sleeves hanging well past her hands. She didn't look at him. Just took a seat in the back and slumped down.

Then came Marcus, shirt untucked, swagger in every step. He stopped in the doorway, looked around like he owned the place, and said, "Ayo, Mr. K, we got more math today?"

The room filled quickly. Mitchell stood in front of the whiteboard, smiling too hard to hide his anxiety. "Good morning, everyone."

No response.

He cleared his throat. "Today we're going to pick up where we left off yesterday, with two-step equations."

A groan. A cough. A wad of paper hit the floor near his foot.

He pressed on, clicking the projector remote. The screen blinked, then went black.

"Seriously?" he muttered.

"Yo, Mr. K can't even work the screen," a student muttered, not even bothering to whisper.

Mitchell turned from the board and saw Jasmine with her head on the desk, Marcus leaning back in his chair, and two boys watching a video on one of their phones.

One girl—without being told—had walked up, grabbed the worksheet from the front table, and was quietly working. That gave him a flicker of hope.

He realized no one else had even picked it up.

He walked down the aisle, trying to force attention through proximity. This time, Marcus didn't say anything. He just grinned.

Mitchell sighed and pivoted. "Okay, let's just try the warm-up on paper," he said, moving toward the whiteboard.

"Everyone grab a sheet from the front table."

He circled back toward Marcus.

"Eyes on your paper, please," Mitchell said.

Marcus smirked. "Can't. Left my eyes at home."

A couple of kids laughed. Mitchell didn't.

He stood at the front again. "Let's try a warm-up together."

A woman poked her head in. "Sorry to interrupt," she said. "I'm looking for one of my students. Is Marcus in here?"

Mitchell looked up, startled. "Uh, not sure. Let me check my attendance sheet."

"Yeah, I'm here," Marcus muttered as he stood to walk out the door.

The door clicked shut. The class exploded.

"What he do?"

"Bro always getting pulled."

"He snuck out yesterday, too."

Mitchell raised a hand. "Alright, that's enough."

No one listened.

He walked over and switched off the projector, jaw tightening. The chatter didn't stop.

He raised his voice. "We're not doing this today."

Still nothing.

Two knocks, then a voice cut through the noise: "Mr. Karns, can I borrow you for a second?"

Tammy stood in the doorway, arms crossed, watching. The room quieted. Not completely, but enough. Mitchell started to offer parting instruction but gave up midsentence as he walked slowly to meet Tammy in the hall.

"You're losing them."

She looked at him, not judging, just seeing. "You alright?" she asked.

He nodded. "Yeah. Just… adjusting."

Tammy raised an eyebrow. "You'll get there. Just don't let the noise make you forget why you're here." Then she was gone.

Mitchell reluctantly returned to class. They were watching him now, waiting to see what he'd do. Whether he'd give up. Whether he'd try too hard. Whether he'd keep pretending to be in charge.

So he did the only thing he could.

He picked up the marker. And started again.

When the bell rang, he stayed in the classroom. He cleaned up papers, realigned chairs, and erased the board. He didn't rush. He wasn't ready to face the hallway.

When he finally stepped out, Tammy was leaning against the lockers. "211 sounded less like a battlefield today," she said.

"Barely."

She nodded. "It takes time."

He was surprised by the softness in her voice. "I don't know if I'm cut out for this."

She shrugged. "Most of us aren't—at first. But kids don't need perfect. They need present."

He looked down the hallway. Kids laughing. Others walking alone. A thousand different stories walking on the same tile floors.

"What do you do when they just… don't care?" he asked.

Tammy glanced at him, her tone shifting to something more reflective. "You know, I had this one student, way back when. Couldn't get him to focus on anything, not English, not anything. He was too busy being mad at the world."

Mitchell looked at her, trying to make sense of what she was getting at.

"His name was Chris," she continued. "And at first, I thought it was me. I thought if I just made the lesson more engaging, more exciting, he'd come around. But every day, he'd tune me out, try to start arguments, get the class riled up."

Mitchell was listening, now leaning in a little, curious.

Tammy smiled lightly, but her eyes were deep in the memory. "One day, I got fed up. It wasn't the lesson that mattered. It was him. So, I told him to stay after class. I asked him what he wanted me to know about him. Not about grammar. Not about the homework. About him. His life. His story."

Mitchell blinked. "Did that work?"

"Not immediately. But over time, it did. You see, when we care about the person, not the problem, things change."

She paused at the door, then added,

"They care. They just don't trust you yet."

Mitchell didn't respond. He ads she walked away, her words echoing behind her like a challenge.

He went back into his classroom, sat down, and stared at the board again. He imagined what his classroom could look like a month from now. A year. He didn't know how to get there yet, but he was willing to try something different.

Not smarter. Not louder. Just *real*.

He pulled out a sticky note and scribbled a reminder in big, uneven letters:

Be the person they need.

He stuck it in the corner of his desk. No one would notice it. But he would. Every day.

He didn't need to be great.

He just needed to be real. To connect.

CHAPTER
3

NOT IN THE BROCHURE

THEY HAD TOLD Mitchell about the curriculum. About standards, assessments, pacing guides. They taught him how to unlock an online gradebook and how to use data to "drive instruction."

But no one told him what to do when emotions got out of hand.

Second period was already a disaster.

The projector still didn't work. Marcus had upped his sarcasm game. Jasmine had fallen asleep. One student openly mocked Mitchell's choice of outfit while another filmed the critique. The room buzzed with side conversations, drumming pencils, whispered curses, and that uniquely middle school tone of performative defiance, loud enough for peers, but just quiet enough to avoid consequences.

Mitchell tried to keep the lesson moving. But every time he asked a question, he was met with blank stares or dramatic groans. At one point, he explained a simple problem four different ways. No one cared.

He felt the familiar wave of heat rise in his chest. That tight, creeping pressure behind his eyes. He was trying, he was really trying. And it still wasn't enough.

Then it happened.

In the back corner, two boys were shoving each other. It wasn't playful. One stood up fast, eyes locked on the other. He reached behind him, grabbed the edge of his chair, and began to lift it off the ground.

Mitchell froze.

A student across the room gasped. The class quieted, not out of respect, but anticipation.

"Put it down." Mitchell's voice cracked as he said it.

The boy paused. The chair hovered. His eyes stayed hard.

Two quick knocks and the door opened. It was Tammy.

She stepped in slowly, scanning the room, saying nothing. She looked directly at the student holding the chair. Her eyes didn't blink. Her body language didn't shift. She didn't raise her voice.

The room stayed silent.

The student lowered the chair and sat back down.

Tammy held his gaze one second longer, then turned to Mitchell.

"I'll stick around for a bit," she said quietly. "You finish the period."

Mitchell gave a small nod. He didn't have the words—but somehow, her presence steadied him.

When the bell rang, students filed out. The tension still hung in the air, but the room was intact. Tammy motioned to Mitchell, and they stepped into the hallway.

It was quiet outside the classroom, but Mitchell's head was still spinning. His thoughts raced in every direction. *What just happened? Why didn't I step up? What's wrong with me?*

Tammy looked at him. "You alright?"

He hesitated. "Honestly? No."

She gave a half-nod. "That's okay. Things can go off the rails fast when you're working with kids. What matters is how you respond—and that takes practice."

Mitchell raised an eyebrow. *Was she serious?* She seemed calm, like this was part of the process.

She leaned against the wall, arms crossed. "There's a moment every new teacher has. Sometimes it's week one, sometimes it's month three. But it always comes. The moment when you realize this isn't about lessons or standards or the syllabus. It's about the weight you carry for kids who carry too much already."

Mitchell looked down the hall. "And when they don't care?"

"They care," she said with a sigh. "They're just testing you. Not to make your life harder, but to see if you'll stick around. They want to know if you'll stay when it gets tough."

Mitchell was quiet. He felt the sting behind his eyes and blinked it back. *Testing me? Why? What do they think I'm supposed to do?*

She sighed again, her voice dropping a bit. "The thing is, there's no magic formula. No one can teach you how to handle that moment. You can't read about it in a book or a pacing guide. All you can do is show up, even when they're pushing you away, even when it feels like you're not getting through to them."

She paused for a second. "You know what I've learned? Connection is often the difference between a teacher burning out… and sparking a fire in their students. Sometimes, it's just that one degree of difference."

Mitchell nodded, absorbing her words. It was so much simpler than what he had been taught in the teacher training seminars. But somehow, it made sense.

Tammy's expression softened, but only slightly. "Every teacher's been there. You freeze, you get frustrated, you want to give up. It's not easy. But the ones who stay? They're the ones who make a difference. It's not the degree, or the training. It's the choice to keep showing up."

He nodded slowly. He was still processing everything. There was so much he didn't know yet.

She gave him a serious look, her voice steady. "Respect doesn't come from a badge or a title. It comes from showing up every day even when they don't make it easy. It comes from sticking around when everyone else might walk away. That's what they need to see from you."

They stood in silence for a few seconds, the weight of her words settling in. The hallway felt oddly empty, though the school around them was bustling. The noise of the students was muffled now, distant. Mitchell's thoughts seemed clearer. He was starting to see what Tammy meant. The quiet moments between them felt powerful, like he could finally hear her message without the noise.

She let the silence linger, then added, "This isn't something they teach you in education programs. Sometimes you learn it the hard way, by freezing, by messing up, by watching someone else step in. It's not the best teacher, but sometimes it's the only one we get.

"You froze a little, but it happens. That's why I stepped in. No shame in that. But now you've seen it. Next time, it's yours."

As Mitchell turned toward the door, she added one more thing, her voice gentle but firm. "Some days, just surviving the day is a win. Don't discount that. We all start there."

Something shifted in him.

They returned to the classroom. Mitchell walked in with more clarity, more breath in his lungs. The chaos didn't magically disappear. But his posture changed. His tone steadied. He started again.

After school, Mitchell sat in his car for fifteen minutes, just breathing. The day hadn't gone well. But something felt different. He hadn't quit. He hadn't stormed out. He'd been rattled, but he'd returned. It wasn't much, but it was something.

He thought about what Tammy had said. About consistency. About staying.

He opened his notebook and wrote it at the top of the next day's plan. Not the objective. Not the standard. Just that one reminder:

Keep showing up.

He paused, then wrote another line below it:

Grace before grades. Patience before programs. Love before lessons.

He didn't know where he had first heard them, but the words felt like oxygen. He felt like he was finally learning to breathe in this space. Grace. Patience. Love. Not things he had thought about before in his training. But it felt right.

He thought about his own teachers. The ones who saw him. Who didn't give up. Who showed up, even when he didn't deserve it. They were the ones who had made a difference in his life, and now, he had the chance to do the same.

He didn't know yet if he was going to be a great teacher.

But today? He survived. And maybe, for now, that was enough.

CHAPTER 4

THE TEACHER ACROSS THE HALL

THE MOMENT HE stepped into Room 211 that morning, bleary-eyed and gripping his coffee tumbler like a lifeline, he noticed her door already open.

And there she was.

Tammy stood just outside Room 212, one hand free for fist bumps, shoulder pats, or quick notes scribbled on the note pad she carried—always watching for who looked off, withdrawn, or just needed to be seen. Each student who walked by got more than a hello.

"Morning, Keon."

"Trinity, those shoes are fire."

"Carlos, everything okay? You look wiped."

Some smiled. Some mumbled. Some just nodded. But all of them were seen.

Mitchell slowed his steps without meaning to. From just inside his own doorway, he watched.

He'd walked by her class a dozen times before. But he hadn't really *seen* it until now.

It wasn't a performance. It was practice.

She wasn't taking attendance. She was taking emotional inventory.

No data wall could capture what she was gathering in three seconds flat—who needed a check-in, who was hyped up, who was already carrying something heavy.

She gave a quiet word to one girl and made a note on a sticky pad.

It was management without barking. Structure without stiffness. And somehow, it worked.

Mitchell blinked, shook himself out of the trance, and decided to pop over and ask Tammy a quick question about lesson pacing.

He stepped into her doorway. Before he could get a word out, her voice stopped him cold.

"Nope. Back out," she said, without even turning. "We have a rule about entering our class: Answer a question first."

He paused, confused. "What?"

Now she looked at him, half-smiling. "You want to enter Room 212, you answer a question first. Standard protocol."

She turned to the class. "Alright team, hit him."

A hand shot up. "Grammar!"

Tammy nodded. "Mitchell, what's the difference between an independent clause and a dependent clause?"

He scratched his head. "… An independent one can stand on its own as a sentence?"

"And the dependent?"

"Needs… more to make sense?"

The kids chuckled.

"Good enough," Tammy said. "There's a bit more nuance to it than that, but close enough. You may enter."

A few students clapped like he'd passed an initiation. Mitchell stepped in, mock-bowing slightly, and several students laughed again.

One leaned over and whispered, "New sub?"

"No," Tammy said without missing a beat. "Mr. Karns teaches across the hall. He's just checking things out."

The student gave him a thumbs-up. "Good luck."

Mitchell grinned, but underneath his freshly pressed sports coat, he was sweating.

What Mitchell quickly learned was that this wasn't just some quirky routine. It was a core part of her philosophy. The entry questions didn't just serve as a "gimmick" or a time-filler. They were part of how she cultivated an environment of trust, respect, and vulnerability in her classroom.

Every adult who entered her room, from administrators to fellow teachers, had to answer a question before being allowed to step through the door.

It wasn't a "test" in the traditional sense. Tammy used it to break the ice and level the playing field. Who wanted to miss a question in front of a room full of students? It made the adults work for it, earn their place, model vulnerability. It was about saying, "I don't know everything, and that's okay." And for the students, it was a reminder that even adults didn't have all the answers. The students loved it. They respected the adults who were willing to show their humanity, and it made them feel like they had a voice in the classroom.

Mitchell didn't intend to stay long in her classroom that day, but he was captivated. He couldn't help but notice the calm authority in Tammy's voice, the way she invited students to engage rather than demanding it. It was natural, as though she had always known how to build trust. But as Mitchell observed, he began to wonder: *How did she get here? How had she learned to embrace vulnerability in a classroom filled with such energy?*

During a quiet moment between lessons, he asked her. "How did you get so good at this?"

Tammy paused, looked at Mitchell, then turned her gaze to the students, still immersed in their work. "I wasn't always like this," she said quietly. "I used to be rigid. I thought control was the key. But the more I focused on getting things perfect, the less I connected with the kids. I remember one year... It was a disaster. No matter how much I planned, how much I structured, nothing worked. I was so focused on the syllabus, the test scores, the grades, that I lost sight of the students."

Mitchell nodded, intrigued. "So, what changed?"

She smiled faintly, as though remembering.

"One day, a student stayed after class. Her name was Jess. I'd asked her to stay because she hadn't turned in an assignment for the third time. She didn't say anything at first, just sat there, looking at the floor. And I realized—she wasn't the problem. I was. I wasn't seeing her, not the way she needed to be seen.

That was the turning point. I started focusing less on perfection and more on relationships. I began to ask questions like 'What's going on with you?' rather than 'Why didn't you turn in your homework?'"

She paused for a moment, then added, "It's like everything else in life, Mitchell. It's about prioritizing. I learned to major on the majors. Teaching wasn't about making everything perfect, but about making sure the kids knew they mattered. And that's what I made my focus, relationships, respect, trust. The rest? It fell into place when I got that right."

After class, as the students filed out, a girl stopped by his desk.

"You're lucky. She's the only teacher who really gets us," she said. "Like the only one who really sees us."

Mitchell didn't know what to say. So he just nodded.

When the room finally quieted, Tammy sat at her desk, looking over some materials. "Well?" she asked, her voice steady but inviting.

"I'm stunned," he said, his voice full of awe.

She raised an eyebrow. "You expected confetti?"

"No," he admitted, "I expected control. But it was something else."

"Trust," she said simply. "And respect. Both earned. Every day."

Mitchell nodded again, slowly. "How long did it take you to build that?"

She shrugged. "Longer than I wanted. Shorter than most think. It's not about tricks. It's about being consistent, clear, and kind. Every time."

Mitchell stood to leave but couldn't tear himself away.

"I learned more in that one class than I have so far in my certification program," he admitted.

Tammy raised an eyebrow. "Because that wasn't a class. That was connection."

He nodded. "It's… humbling."

"Good. Humble teachers grow. Proud ones cling to their ways. And students always know the difference."

Mitchell paused in the doorway. "Can I come again?"

"You'd be a fool not to," she said, smirking.

He stepped back into the hallway, Tammy's classroom air still in his lungs. The energy was still palpable, alive with purpose. There was something about the way Tammy created an environment where students weren't just "listening." They were active participants.

For a moment, Mitchell stood in the hallway, taking it all in. Inside Room 212, a student nailed an answer, and the class lit up.

Tammy grinned and gave the student a high-five. "We work hard, and we play hard," she said, her voice full of energy. "That's how we do it in here."

Mitchell smiled. It wasn't just a motto. It was a mindset. A way of teaching. A way of being.

He returned to Room 211 and sat at his desk. The silence felt heavier now—not in a burdensome way, but like a space waiting to be filled.

He opened his notebook and wrote at the top of a fresh page:

The classroom isn't about compliance. It's about connection.

He underlined it twice, then added something Tammy hadn't said, but that was ringing in his ears:

Some of the best professional development is the teacher down the hall.

And just before closing it, he wrote one more line:

Room 212 isn't just a room. It's a reminder of who I want to be.

Because Tammy wasn't just the teacher across the hall. She was the kind of teacher every school needs. The one who doesn't just make kids better, but makes teachers better, too.

A mentor.

A leader.

The extra degree.

CHAPTER

5

THE
OBSERVATION

It was Mitchell's planning period, and he had arranged ahead of time to observe Tammy's class. After a rough second period where over half the class disengaged, two kids walked out claiming to need the nurse, and Marcus pretended to fall asleep mid-instruction, Mitchell found himself standing outside Room 212.

Her door was open, like always. Jazz murmured from an old speaker. The lights were dimmed slightly, sunlight filtering through thin curtains. It didn't look like a classroom. It looked like a place people wanted to be.

Mitchell knocked once.

Tammy glanced up from her desk, then back down at a stack of index cards. "You're early. Sit in the back. No rescuing."

"No rescuing?" he echoed.

"If I call on you, you answer. No passes for grown-ups."

He nodded and made his way to the last desk in the row by the window.

The class was already settling in. A few students looked up but didn't say much. It wasn't a performance for him. It was just how the room ran.

Mitchell opened his notebook and took a breath.

This was the observation. But it didn't feel like one.

It felt like walking into something alive.

Tammy began class without raising her voice. No shouting, no desperate attempts at silence, just posture, presence, and rhythm. She didn't wait for complete silence. She assumed it. And when one student whispered, she paused, not angry, not impatient. Just paused. The student noticed. The room corrected itself.

"Today's warm-up," she said, "is written on the board. Copy it, answer it, and explain why you think your answer is right. If you finish early, you're probably wrong."

A few students chuckled.

Mitchell watched as the class leaned in. Not slumped. Not resistant. Engaged.

She weaved through desks without saying a word. A tap on the shoulder here, a nod there. She handed out nothing and somehow gave everything. Every movement felt deliberate, every touch a quiet reminder that this was her space, but they were part of it, too.

There was something unspoken in the room, a subtle acknowledgment of shared responsibility. Tammy didn't have to demand attention. She commanded it by being fully present.

After ten minutes, she clapped once.

"Let's talk about the first sentence. Jada, can you read yours?"

Jada confidently read her response.

"Who disagrees with Jada?"

Three hands shot up.

Tammy continued, maintaining that sense of space. Every move purposeful, every question layered. It wasn't about finding the "right" answer. It was about the process of thinking, debating, and growing.

Mitchell looked around and saw students checking each other's papers, debating ideas, not yelling over who was right, but discussing why something was right. It was a level of engagement he hadn't anticipated.

He felt something tighten in his chest.

It wasn't jealousy. It wasn't envy. It was clarity.

This was what he had imagined teaching would feel like. Not perfect. Not silent. But alive. The room was breathing. Students weren't being "taught." They were learning.

Mitchell remembered what Tammy had shared the day before about her early years of rigid control, rule charts, and chasing perfection. How it all began to change with one quiet student who didn't need discipline, just to be seen.

During a lull between activities, he leaned in. "So... how did you figure this out?"

Tammy paused, watching the students work quietly at their desks, then turned to him.

"I stopped trying to control them," she said. "And started teaching them how to control themselves."

She leaned back slightly, her voice calm.

"Rules matter. But when they're the centerpiece of your classroom, you're always reacting. You end up policing behavior instead of building people."

Mitchell nodded slowly.

Tammy continued, "The shift came when I started teaching routines. Predictability. Emotional regulation. Community. I stopped asking, 'How do I get them to behave?' and started asking, 'What kind of environment helps them thrive?'"

She smiled faintly. "My classroom became a training ground. For kindness. For focus. For trust. That's what school should be, not just learning what not to do, but how to show up better."

She hesitated for a moment, then added, "You ever heard the 212-degree thing?"

Mitchell shook his head.

"At 211 degrees, water is hot," she said. "At 212? It boils. Boiling water makes steam. And steam moves things. It can even power engines."

She let the silence linger. "That single degree makes all the difference."

Mitchell nodded slowly. "So why does that matter to you?"

Tammy looked toward the window. "Because I used to live at 211. I did everything right. Checked all the boxes. Ran a tight ship. But nothing moved, not the kids, not me. And then one day, after I snapped on a student for something small, my mentor left a note on my desk. It just said, 'You're one degree away.'"

She turned back to him. "That broke me. But it also rewired me. I realized it wasn't about being more perfect. It was about being more present. Having one degree more patience. One degree more belief. One degree more grace even if the kid hadn't earned it yet."

She paused, her voice even softer now.

"Anyone can be in the room. But being present? That's different. That's leaning in. Paying attention. Choosing to care out loud. That's the one degree that changes everything."

Mitchell didn't speak. He didn't need to. He just nodded, quietly absorbing the weight of what she'd said.

Back in Room 211, he sat at his desk without opening his notebook. No strategies. No checklist. Just a thought that wouldn't leave him:

Presence doesn't shout. It steadies. It grounds. It invites.

And for the first time, he understood.

The one degree isn't something you do. It's something you become.

He peered into the hallway that separated his room from Tammy's. A gap that once felt like miles.

Today, it felt like a bridge.

WHY ARE YOU REALLY HERE?

It HAD BEEN three weeks since the first day.

Mitchell sat at his desk, staring at the stack of ungraded quizzes. The classroom felt silent, even though the building hummed with the usual school sounds.

He was tired—exhausted in a way that had nothing to do with lesson planning. It was the kind of tired that made him question everything.

Since that first week, he'd tried. He'd greeted students at the door. He'd used a few of Tammy's lines— *"What's going on with you?"* instead of *"Where's your homework?"* He'd made space for check-ins, slowed his pacing, even started using a reset zone.

But still, most days felt like chaos barely contained. The connection he was chasing still felt out of reach.

He had started this journey with a vision: to help kids, to make an impact.

But right now, it still felt like he was just trying to survive.

Knock. Knock.

Tammy appeared in the doorway, holding two steaming cups of coffee.

"Black, right?" she asked, a small smile on her lips.

He nodded, surprised. "You didn't have to."

"I didn't," she said, stepping inside with an easy confidence. "But I did anyway."

She handed him the cup and sat across from him. He took a sip, the warmth settling in his chest. "Is this... actually good?"

Tammy smirked. "Shockingly, yes. The principal believes in taking care of her people. Good coffee, stocked fridge, real creamer—the lounge isn't a punishment."

He chuckled, but the tension in his shoulders didn't ease. "In my last job, the breakroom had a microwave from 1994 and a passive-aggressive note about time management."

Tammy smiled knowingly. "Yeah, well, here the coffee's decent and the snacks are stocked. The work still finds a way to wear you down. But little things matter."

She tilted her head, her gaze steady. "You alright?"

Mitchell hesitated. It wasn't just about the quizzes. He wasn't sure if he even remembered what had drawn him into teaching anymore. The disillusionment was heavier than any stack of papers.

"I'm not sure anymore," he admitted quietly.

Tammy crossed her arms thoughtfully. "You ever ask yourself why you're really here?"

Mitchell blinked, caught off guard. "You mean today?"

"No," she murmured. "I mean here. This building. This job. These kids."

Her question hung in the air. Was he here to *fix something*? To prove to himself that he could be a good teacher? Or was there something more?

She didn't give him time to answer, her words filling the space between them. "You know, Mitchell, a lot of people come into teaching thinking they're here to save kids. Or fix the system. Or prove something to themselves. But teaching burns off those illusions quickly. What's left is the truth. And sometimes… that truth isn't as pretty as we think it is."

Mitchell stared into his coffee, feeling his idealism crumble. The vision he had held of himself—of how impactful he thought his work could be—wasn't matching up with the reality of the classroom. It wasn't about changing the world in a day. It was about the slow, sometimes painful work of showing up every day, even when it felt like nothing was getting through.

"I thought I could make a difference," he said quietly.

Tammy nodded, her gaze warm. "Good. But whose difference? Yours? Or theirs?"

Mitchell didn't have an answer.

"I've seen a lot of teachers come through this hallway," she continued. "Some brilliant, some passionate. But the ones who last? They're the ones who stop performing and start listening. The ones who realize this isn't about being liked, it's about being real."

She leaned forward, her eyes focused on him. "You know what the job really is, Mitchell? It's about being the adult who doesn't walk away. Who shows up when they don't have to. Who holds the line when everything else in a kid's life is chaos."

Mitchell felt her words settle deep within him. *This* was the job—showing up, not for the accolades, not for perfection, but for the students who needed him to simply be there.

"I just…" he trailed off, his voice breaking. "I didn't think it would be this hard."

"Of course you didn't," Tammy said gently. "None of us do. We come in thinking it's about lessons, about test scores, about behavior. And then we meet the real job—the emotional weight, the heartbreak, the thousand silent stories sitting in those desks."

She let the silence linger for a moment. "You're going to have days where you question everything. Days where you feel like nothing you're doing matters. But it does. Even if they don't show it right away."

Mitchell exhaled, the heaviness still pressing on him. "I feel like I'm failing them."

"No," Tammy said firmly. "You're just still finding your why."

He glanced around his classroom. The sterile walls, the lifeless space—designed for management, but not for connection.

Tammy noticed his gaze. "When I first started, I had motivational quotes printed on every wall. I thought if I looked the part, I'd feel the part. But those words didn't make me a good teacher. What did? Learning their names. Noticing their moods. Giving second chances. Showing up when I didn't feel like it."

"I'm not sure I know how to do all that," he admitted.

"You will," she said. "But only if you're honest with yourself first. Why are you here? Really?"

He looked at her, the weight of the question sinking in. "Because I thought I had more to give."

Tammy nodded slowly. "Then give it. Not your perfection. Not your performance. Just your presence. Your attention. That's what they'll remember."

She stood to leave but paused at the door. "You can't give what you don't have," she said, her voice gentle but firm. "So take care of yourself. Reflect. Get clear." She lingered for a moment longer. "So many teachers try to do it all. They don't set boundaries. But boundaries aren't about doing less or chasing balance. They're about setting priorities. And if you don't protect your priorities, the job will eat you alive."

She walked out, leaving him with more questions than answers.

That night, Mitchell didn't touch his lesson plans.

He didn't check emails.

He didn't scroll social media.

He sat alone in the quiet, a single lamp glowing beside him, and opened his journal to a blank page.

Across the top, he wrote just one question:

Why are you really here?

He stared at it for a long time.

Not expecting an answer—just listening for it.

The silence didn't feel empty, it felt expectant.

Like something he'd ignored for far too long was finally ready to speak.

He thought about Mrs. Caldwell, his seventh-grade teacher—the one who noticed him. She never let him skip class, even when he hated it. But she let him eat lunch in her room, no questions asked. She saw that he didn't need discipline. He needed safety.

He thought about the day his daughter Emma looked up at him from the passenger seat and said, "You don't seem happy anymore." Not accusing. Just observing. Like a mirror he hadn't wanted to face.

He thought about that sterile conference room—the hum of false importance in every word. Margins. Markets. Models. He remembered watching people talk with urgency about things that didn't matter, and realizing his soul was starving for meaning. The layoff didn't break him, it released him. It wasn't the door closing that shook him.

It was the quiet voice underneath it all whispering, *Now. Now you can finally go where you were always meant to.*

For the first time, he let himself believe that maybe he had never been off track. Maybe he had just taken the long road to where he truly belonged.

He thought about the students he hadn't met yet.

The ones who rolled their eyes so they wouldn't have to show fear. The ones who made jokes because crying was too dangerous. The ones whose silence said more than their words ever could.

And then he wrote—slowly, carefully:

To be the person I needed.

To be the person they *need.*

To love what I teach. But love who *I teach more.*

He sat back, pen resting in his hand. Those words weren't polished. They weren't profound.

But they were the truest thing he'd written in years.

This—*this*—was the calling he had ignored.

Not a job.

A vow.

Not to be a perfect teacher, but to be a steady one.

Present. Real. Human.

Tammy's words echoed back: "Teaching burns off your illusions until only the truth remains."

And the truth was simple. He didn't have all the answers. He probably never would.

But maybe that wasn't the point.

Maybe the point was to keep showing up anyway. To offer presence over perfection. To give what he had—until it became what someone else needed.

The next morning, he walked into Room 211 feeling energized. Awake.

Tammy passed him in the hallway.

"You look taller today."

He smiled. "Might be the coffee."

She stopped, looked at him just long enough to see past the joke. "Might be the clarity."

He turned to keep walking, but her voice stopped him.

"You know why I'm still here?" she asked, almost absently. "In this old building, in this same room, after all these years?"

He glanced back. She wasn't waiting for an answer.

"It's not because I've figured it all out," she said. "It's because every year, one kid walks through that door who needs someone to believe in them before they believe in themselves. That's the job. That's why."

She paused, then added, "They don't just need a good curriculum. Or the newest tech. They need someone who sees them—who believes in who they *could* become, not just who they are right now. That belief? It's what makes everything else matter."

She smiled knowingly—and disappeared into Room 212.

Mitchell stood there a moment longer.

He wasn't chasing certainty anymore. He was walking into something deeper.

It was about remembering *why* you keep showing up.

And doing it—on purpose.

YOU DON'T TEACH CONTENT. YOU TEACH HUMANS.

THE MORNING BUZZED like it always did, hallways filled with chatter, sneakers squeaking on tile, and doors slamming just a little too loudly. Mitchell stepped into Room 211 with a nod to the custodian, clutching his coffee like a lifeline. His lesson plan sat neatly on the desk: linear equations, group practice, exit ticket. All the boxes checked. All the standards met.

But something in him knew that today wasn't about equations.

He walked to the front of the room and set his coffee down. As students shuffled in, some avoiding eye contact, others too tired to pretend to care, he felt that unspoken truth in the air. Today wasn't about content. It was about *connection*.

Marcus tossed his backpack across the room and missed the hook as usual. Jasmine stared out the window like it owed her an answer. Another girl in the front row kept rubbing her temples, already overwhelmed before a word had been said.

Mitchell had the content. He had the pacing. But what he didn't have yet was their hearts.

Halfway through first period, he abandoned the group work. Something told him to just ask a question.

"How many of you have had a rough morning?"

Ten hands went up.

"How many of you have ever felt like school doesn't really get you?"

Twelve hands this time. A few eyes shifted. A few heads nodded.

Mitchell exhaled. "Okay. Then today, let's talk about what it would take to change that."

The room shifted. The tension cracked.

Jasmine looked up. Marcus sat straighter. For the first time that week, they weren't just students. They were humans. Seen. Heard.

He wrote nothing on the board for the next thirty minutes. They talked. Not about math. About mornings. About things that made them feel invisible. About the pressure to pretend nothing's wrong. And Mitchell listened, not to fix, not to manage. Just to understand.

Then Jasmine raised her hand. "Can we help set the vibe for this class?"

Mitchell blinked. "You want to create the expectations?"

Marcus shrugged. "If we're supposed to follow them, we should have a say."

A few others spoke in agreement.

Mitchell looked around the room. Students who had just days ago barely looked up were now leaning in, ready to help build something better.

He nodded. "Alright. Tomorrow, we start writing the next chapter together."

As Mitchell sat there, watching his students take ownership, not just of their stories, but of the classroom itself, something inside him began to shift. His previous days had been filled with frustration, not because the kids didn't care, but because he hadn't truly *seen them*. He had been so focused on the lessons and the content, the stuff he was supposed to deliver, that he had missed the most important part—*who they were.*

In that moment, as they became less like a teacher and his students and more like two groups trying to understand each other, Mitchell began to feel what he had been missing. *Connection.*

Later that day, in the teacher's lounge, Mitchell found Tammy refilling her mug, still calm despite the chaos of the morning.

"You look like you saw a ghost," she said, glancing at him.

"Worse," he replied. "I saw my lesson plan go out the window."

Tammy chuckled, an understanding glint in her eye. "Good. That means you're actually teaching."

He raised an eyebrow.

"Teaching isn't delivering content," she said. "It's knowing when content needs to wait because the humans in your room are falling apart."

Mitchell sipped his coffee. "Why doesn't anyone say that in training?"

"Because no one wants to admit how messy it really is. But here's the truth: You don't teach math, or science, or writing. You teach kids. Some come with trauma. Some come with anger. Some just have no idea how to handle the world yet."

He nodded, the weight of her words sinking in. "And yet we expect them to handle everything perfectly."

"Exactly," Tammy said. "We say they should know better. But did anyone teach them better?"

He looked down at his own mug, the warmth now comforting, but the truth still pressing on him.

"You can teach math," she added. "But if you don't teach trust, boundaries, respect. The math won't matter."

Mitchell paused. "I guess I've been focusing more on the lessons than the learners."

"Most of us do at first," she said. "But the best teachers? They get it. They learn to lead hearts before they lead minds."

He thought about his daughter, Emma, and what she had said

before he started teaching: "Just listen to them. That's what makes the good ones."

Tammy stood, adjusting her jacket. "You're not here to deliver content. You're here to help students become the best version of themselves. But to do that, you have to see the kid first, not the subject."

He nodded slowly, absorbing her words. "So how do I do that?"

"Start with curiosity. Keep showing up. And remember connection before curriculum. Always."

She paused. "It's easy to teach content. It takes everything to teach humans."

She turned back with a final word: "And remember, Mitchell. Students don't remember the worksheet. They remember how you made them feel when they didn't have the words for what they were going through."

Mitchell sat with her words long after she left. Then he returned to his room.

He crossed out the day's learning target in his binder. Underneath, he wrote:

Today's objective: Build trust. Show them they matter.

The bell rang. Students walked in.

Mitchell didn't rush to the lesson.

He greeted each student by name. Asked how their morning was. Let the silence stretch just a little longer than usual. As he welcomed them at the door and let them know he was glad they were there, he realized that might just be one of the most important parts of the school day.

For the first time, he wasn't just teaching.

He was reaching out, meeting them where and how they were.

And maybe, just maybe, that's where real learning starts.

CHAPTER

8

THE PROBLEM ISN'T THE KIDS

IT WAS ONE of those mornings when Mitchell's patience was already frayed before the first bell rang. A student had launched a pencil across the room during homeroom. Another showed up without a backpack for the third time that week. And Marcus, stretching across two desks, announced to anyone who'd listen that math was "a government conspiracy to control our minds."

Mitchell tried to shake it off. Tried to remember Tammy's words. But by the time third period ended, his optimism had evaporated. It felt like he was spending more energy managing chaos than teaching anything at all.

Later that afternoon, after the final bell had rung and the building had started to empty out, Mitchell found himself in the teachers' lounge. Not for coffee this time, just to collect himself. To take a breath. The room was quiet, filled only with the soft hum of the vending machine and the faint clink of a spoon against ceramic.

Tammy stood at the counter, stirring her mug, calm as ever. This time, she refrained from speaking first.

"I don't think these kids are teachable," Mitchell muttered, not looking up.

She raised an eyebrow. "Oh, you're there already?"

He sighed. "What do you mean?"

"The moment you decide it's them, not you."

"I just… I do," he stammered. "I plan, I show up, I follow everything in the book. And still… they don't listen. They don't care."

Tammy took a slow sip. "Some of them are carrying more than you know. Some are testing you. And some are just kids who haven't learned how to regulate anything yet."

"I get the trauma stuff," Mitchell said. "But it's not always trauma. Some of them just… I don't know. Some of them are just wired different."

"Sure," Tammy nodded. "Some are naturally more disagreeable. Some impulsive. Some are angry. But just like we teach content, we can teach behavior. We can model self-control. We can guide emotional regulation. And more importantly, we should."

Mitchell looked up. "We should treat behavior like a subject?"

"I'm saying we should stop assuming they already know what we've never taught."

The hum of the vending machine filled the pause.

"We teach kids how to multiply fractions or structure a sentence," she continued. "But do we teach them how to apologize? How to respectfully advocate for themselves? How to recognize when they're about to lose it and take a second instead?"

Mitchell nodded slowly. "I never learned any of that growing up. Not in school."

"Exactly," she said. "And here we are expecting them to demonstrate behaviors we're still learning ourselves."

He let the words settle in thoughtful quiet.

"You know," Tammy added, "teachers burn out not just from workload but from trying to control what's out of their control. So many try to do it all, but not everything's urgent. The key is to focus on what matters most. Sometimes, that means giving kids the freedom to move rather than punishing them for wiggling in their seats."

He smiled. "I actually started something this week," he said, leaning forward. "A shift in how I think about behavior—and how students experience my classroom. I cleared out a corner and created something I call the *reset zone*. It's not a punishment. Not a time-out. It's a pause. A space to breathe, to stretch. There's a mat and even a sign that says, 'Need a second? Take it.'

"It's not just about movement," he continued. "It's a mental and emotional breather. A chance to reset without checking out.

Tammy turned fully toward him. "That's brilliant," she said. "You didn't just clear a corner. You created capacity. You're teaching them what every adult wishes they'd learned: how to recognize their limits and reset with dignity. That's so much more than just social-emotional learning. That's leadership."

"I wasn't sure at first," he admitted. "But they've started using it on their own. No permission, no disruption. Just… self-regulation."

"Exactly," she said. "You created a space for emotional ownership. That's empowering."

Mitchell leaned back. "Rules never really worked for me. But this… this feels different."

Tammy nodded. "Good teachers manage behavior. Great teachers teach routines. The best? They teach responsibility."

Mitchell nodded again, slower this time.

"We're not here to control," she added. "We're here to build systems students can count on. When they know what to expect, they feel safe. And when they feel safe, they can learn."

He exhaled. "So much of what matters isn't in the curriculum."

"Nope. But it's the part they'll remember."

She rinsed her mug and started for the door.

Mitchell called out. "You said they're not unteachable. Just unconvinced?"

Tammy paused. "Exactly. Remember, they're waiting to see if you'll stay. If you're worth trusting. If you see them as more than the messy moments."

He nodded, watching her leave. Then he returned to Room 211.

The reset zone sat in the corner. The lights were dimmed slightly, the room unusually quiet. The area was empty, but its presence had changed something not just in the students but in him.

He walked over to his desk, opened his drawer, and pulled out a sticky note. Without overthinking it, he wrote:

Structure invites calm. Connection sustains it.

He paused. Then added:

They're not broken. They're becoming.

And finally:

They're not unteachable. They're just unconvinced. Show them you're going to keep showing up.

He stuck the note where only he could see it.

Because this was more than classroom management.

This was education.

And it was working.

He didn't overhaul the curriculum. He didn't redesign the classroom. He just made space.

One quiet corner. One clear invitation. One subtle shift from control to trust.

That's what the extra degree looks like—it doesn't demand attention.

It creates it.

CONTROL
VERSUS CONNECTION

MITCHELL HAD ALWAYS believed discipline was about control. Rules. Procedures. Consequences. That's what the trainings said, anyway.

"Students need structure."

"Consistency is key."

"Don't let them see you lose control."

So, he followed the script. Laid down the rules. Posted them on the wall. Enforced them like a sheriff.

But something about that had never felt right.

Now, a few months into the school year, something was starting to click—and it wasn't about control. His classroom wasn't perfect, but it was changing. And so was he.

The reset zone had become part of their rhythm. It wasn't a novelty or a loophole. It was part of the routine. Students used it without asking. They tapped their desks, nodded, and took a moment. They stretched, breathed, reset. And then they came back.

It wasn't about escaping accountability.

It was about owning it.

One morning, Mitchell stood at the front of the room and watched Marcus walk quietly over to the mat. No eye roll. No attitude. Marcus just needed a minute, and he took it. A few deep breaths. A drink of water. Then back to work.

There was no power struggle. No standoff.

Just awareness. And choice.

And Mitchell realized something. He wasn't managing behavior anymore.

He was mentoring growth.

Later that afternoon, Jasmine lingered after class. She hadn't said much all year until now.

"That reset thing," she said, not quite looking at him. "It helps. I don't like talking when I'm mad. But I don't want to blow up either."

He nodded, surprised. "I'm glad you're using it."

She shrugged. "It's better than getting sent out."

That short exchange stayed with him. Not because it was profound, but because it was honest. It was what every training manual skipped: Students weren't problems to fix. They were people trying to manage what the world kept throwing at them.

That evening, as he jotted down notes from the day, Mitchell caught himself writing the phrase:

They're not trying to escape. They're trying to stay regulated.

He stared at it for a moment. That's what Tammy had been showing him all along. Not with a PowerPoint or a program, but through presence. Through the way she structured her classroom like a community, not a command post.

The next day, during his planning period, he found her in the lounge.

"When did it stop being about rules for you?" he asked.

She didn't hesitate. "When I realized rules only tell kids what *not* to do. They don't teach what *to* do."

He nodded. "I used to think I had to run my room like a sheriff, enforce every rule, every time. Make an example out of anyone who stepped out of line."

Tammy raised an eyebrow. "How'd that work out for you?"

He laughed. "Let's just say... I wrote a lot of referrals."

"Because you were reacting," she said. "Not leading."

Mitchell leaned back in his chair. "Yeah. I'm starting to see that now. The reset zone? It's not really about the mat or the sign. It's about trust. It's about giving them responsibility instead of taking all the control."

"Exactly," she said. "Great teachers spend less time policing rules and more time teaching routines, setting expectations, and building responsibility."

She sipped her tea and continued, "You can spend all your time chasing compliance. Or you can build a culture where students learn to manage themselves."

Mitchell nodded. "Structure matters. But without connection, it's just noise."

"Right. Kids don't remember your rules. They remember how you made them feel when they made a mistake and how you helped them come back from it."

Later that night, Mitchell sat at his desk, reflecting. He had spent the first few months of school trying to avoid chaos. He thought control would keep things from unraveling. But now, he realized that *connection* was the anchor. Routines weren't about managing behavior. They were about building confidence. Ownership.

He opened his notebook and wrote:

Rules tell students what not *to do. Routines show them what* to *do.*

Expectations build trust.

Responsibility builds character.

He thought back to a training he once sat through where the speaker said, "Be firm. Be consistent. Don't let them win." But in this moment, Mitchell saw it differently.

This wasn't about winning or losing. It was about *leading*. And growth didn't happen through fear. It happened through safety, structure, and trust.

The next morning, during homeroom, he shared something different with his students.

"I've realized something," he told them. "When I started teaching, I thought the most important thing was rules and making sure everyone followed them. But now I think it's more about routines and expectations. Things that help us grow, not just behave."

They stared at him, unsure where he was going.

"I'm not going to stop having rules," he said, "but I want you to know I trust you to take responsibility for yourselves. That's what the reset zone is about. That's what this whole classroom is about. We're building something here, and it starts with trust."

No one clapped. No big speech. But Mitchell saw it in their faces, the surprise, the curiosity, and maybe even a little respect.

Jasmine gave him the smallest nod. Marcus actually opened his notebook.

It wasn't about perfection. It was about presence.

And they were starting to feel it.

That afternoon, as students packed up for the day, Marcus paused at the door. "Hey, Karns," he said. "You spelled *responsibility* wrong on the board."

Mitchell turned. "Seriously?"

"Yeah," Marcus smirked. "No biggie. I got it."

He grabbed a whiteboard marker and quickly wrote over Mitchell's mistake on his way out the door.

Mitchell just shook his head and smiled.

He glanced around the room, at the desks, the calm, the quiet routines now guiding the day. It wasn't flawless. But it didn't need to be.

The classroom wasn't run by control anymore.

It was led by connection. And trust. And growth.

He was no longer trying to survive the job.

He was becoming the teacher his students needed most.

CHAPTER

10

RELATIONSHIPS
BEFORE RIGOR

MITCHELL SAT AT his desk after school, his eyes blurry from staring at lesson plans that felt irrelevant. The test scores were low. The pressure from administration was high. And everywhere he turned, there was another reminder that rigor was the buzzword of the year. Rigorous standards. Rigorous instruction. Rigorous assessment.

But no one had yet explained how to be rigorous with a room full of students who didn't fully trust you yet.

Tammy knocked twice on the open door to Room 211. In her hand, she held a dry-erase marker. Without saying a word, she walked to his whiteboard and wrote in clean, block letters:

Rigor without relationship leads to resistance.

She capped the marker and faced him. "That's not mine. It's been around for years. But it's still true."

Mitchell raised an eyebrow. "Here to coach me again?"

Tammy smiled. "I'm here because I know the look of a teacher who's doing everything right and still losing sleep."

He leaned back in his chair. "I feel like I'm constantly choosing between covering content and actually reaching them."

Tammy pulled up a student chair and sat. "You can't teach content until you've taught connection. Kids learn better from people they trust."

Mitchell nodded. "I know. I just keep hearing that we need more rigor. More accountability."

"Accountability without empathy is just pressure," Tammy said. "And pressure without trust makes kids shut down."

He looked at the quote on the board again. "So, what do I do tomorrow when I have to introduce fractions and half of them still struggle with multiplication?"

"You slow down," she said. "You go deep instead of wide. You tell them, 'We're going to tackle this together.' And then you look for the small wins even if they're not necessarily academic. When a student who never raises their hand finally does. When someone asks a question instead of giving up."

She paused. "See, relationships aren't just about warm fuzzies and feelings. That's what people get wrong. Classroom relationships are hard. They come with expectations. Accountability. Boundaries. Just like any real relationship, they take work. But when you build them, people rise to meet them. That's where real rigor begins."

Mitchell tapped his fingers on the desk. "So you're saying that rigor starts with students and not standards."

"Exactly," Tammy said. "Students work harder for adults who believe in them. When they know you're invested in their success, they begin to invest too. Rigor grows out of relationship. It never precedes it."

She stood and walked toward the door. "Just remember: You don't teach content. You teach humans. And they don't care what you know until they know you care."

The next morning, Mitchell erased part of his agenda and replaced it with something new. At the top of the board, in big letters, he wrote:

Let's get better together.

Instead of diving straight into the standard, he started with a check-in. One question: "How are you doing today?"

Some students shrugged. Some rolled their eyes. But a few answered honestly.

"Tired."

"Hungry."

"Stressed."

He thanked them for their responses. No fixing. Just listening.

Then he taught fractions but approached it differently. He used examples from their world. Cut a granola bar in half. Talked about sneakers on sale. He slowed the pacing. Let them work in pairs. Gave them space to talk through mistakes.

And something shifted. Not magically. But meaningfully.

Later that week, Jasmine left a folded note on his desk. Inside, in crooked handwriting, it said:

Thanks for not giving up on me. I hated math and still kinda do. But now I feel like I can do some of it.

He sat with that for a long time.

That night, Mitchell opened his laptop to revise his lesson plans. But instead, he opened a new document and titled it:

Human First. Teacher Second.

He began listing the names of students who'd had small victories. Jasmine, who stayed after class to ask for help. Marcus, who actually turned in homework. Camila, who smiled for the first time all year.

These weren't data points. They were reminders.

Rigor wasn't dead. But it wasn't the driver anymore. Relationship was.

And then came a thought. It hit so hard he stopped typing and whispered it out loud:

"If students never experience success in school, why would they believe success is possible in life?"

He stared at the screen, letting it sink in.

"Start with their strengths. That's where confidence begins."

He leaned back in his chair and exhaled. That was it. That was the thing no training had taught him. His job was more than just believing in his students. It was to get them to believe in themselves.

The following week, Mitchell stood at his door and greeted each student by name. He realized something important as he smiled and said good morning: This was more than a greeting. It was a welcome. Each name, each greeting, was a way to say, "You belong here. I'm glad you came." It wasn't magic, but it mattered.

As the days passed, his classroom didn't get quieter, but it got safer. More honest. Students felt the shift, too. And they responded positively.

During group work, students who used to hide behind silence started offering ideas. Mistakes were met with curiosity instead of groans. "Why do you think that didn't work?" became a common phrase. Mitchell encouraged peer support and coaching. He let students explain math problems to each other, and the results stunned him.

By Thursday, Mitchell noticed Jasmine helping another student after finishing early.

"That's actually how I learned it," she told her classmate, sketching it out on paper.

It wasn't perfect. But it was progress. And more than anything, it was proof: relationship created space for growth.

At lunch, Mitchell sat with a few students at a corner table. No agenda. Just presence. One student asked if teachers had favorite students. Mitchell paused, then answered, "We have students who make us better teachers. And that's kind of the same thing."

Later that day, Tammy peeked into his room and raised a brow. "You look a little more at ease."

He nodded. "I stopped trying to cover everything. And started trying to reach everyone."

Tammy smiled. "Now you're teaching."

Mitchell sat at his kitchen table that night, the hum of the dishwasher in the background, his laptop open but untouched. He had papers to grade, emails to return. But his mind kept circling one thought.

He reached for a sticky note and jotted it down:

You can't force kids to care about content. But if they know you care about them, they'll try harder than you ever expected.

He pondered another moment, then wrote second line beneath it:

Learning isn't something you pour into them. It's something you pull out. And when that happens, rigor is never far behind.

He thought about the quiz from earlier that day. The scores weren't perfect. But the effort? It was different. Focused. Intentional. One student had even written under their answer:

I don't think I got it, but I tried. Please don't mark it wrong if it's not right.

Mitchell smiled when he remembered what he'd written back:

Trying matters. Come see me. We'll work on it together.

And that Thursday, the student had asked for help.

He glanced around the quiet kitchen, then added one more line to the note:

Rigor grows when students feel safe, seen, and connected to what they're learning, especially when it connects to what they're good at or what they care about.

He leaned back and exhaled.

This wasn't the kind of insight that came from training modules or strategy binders. It came from showing up. From noticing. From caring.

He thought about Jasmine using the reset zone without prompting. About Marcus turning in a completed assignment without a snide remark. About how the classroom no longer felt like something he had to control, but something he was beginning to cultivate.

It hit him all at once:

You can spend your time enforcing rules like a sheriff, or you can spend your energy building routines, setting expectations, and teaching responsibility.

One controls behavior.

The other shapes character.

He stared at those words for a long time.

That was the shift.

Raising the relationship without lowering the bar.

CHAPTER

11

THE TABLE IN
THE CORNER

AT FIRST, IT was just a place to sit.

The cafeteria was loud. It always was. But Mitchell wasn't avoiding the noise that day. He just wanted to observe. Something had shifted in him since the conversation with Tammy about seeing students. He was starting to notice the invisible things. The corners. The kids no one talked to. The quiet spaces where stories lived.

That's what drew his eyes to the table in the far corner.

Four students. No eye contact. No noise. They weren't in trouble, but they weren't included either. It was unofficially known as "the peanut table." That title had once referred to the table being set apart due to allergies, but now, it had become code for kids who didn't belong anywhere else.

Mitchell didn't hesitate. He grabbed his lunch and sat down.

Heads turned throughout the entire cafeteria.

One student squinted. "Uh… you know this is the weird table, right?"

Mitchell smiled. "Guess I'm in the right place, then."

He didn't lead a conversation. He just ate. Asked a few questions. Laughed when someone made a joke about the mystery meat. By the end of lunch, no one had really opened up. But something had shifted. A crack, small but real.

He came back the next day. And the next. No clipboard. No discipline referrals. Just presence.

That's when they started talking. First in fragments. Then in full thoughts.

"Mr. K, you watch anime?"

"What music did you like when you were in middle school?"

"You ever heard of Minecraft?"

He answered honestly. Sometimes awkwardly. And he asked back.

"What's something people don't know about you?"

"Why do you think people sit here?"

One student shrugged. "Because people like to know where to look when they want to ignore you."

That line stayed with him.

The following week, Jasmine slid a folded piece of paper across the table. On it was a short poem—funny, sarcastic, and sharp. He read it twice.

"You wrote this?"

She nodded, brushing it off. "Just something I was messing with."

"It's not just something," he said. "It's something you should share."

He leaned back. "You know... I used to be the kid at the quiet table too. I didn't fit in. I was obsessed with numbers and puzzles, and I never knew what to say at lunch."

Jasmine smirked. "So not much has changed?"

He laughed. "Not really."

Then he added, "But the thing is, being different doesn't mean being less. It just means you have strengths other people haven't seen the value in yet."

He looked around the table. "All of you have something the world needs. You just might not know it yet."

Another student asked, "Like what if we made a space to show it?"

Mitchell smiled. "Exactly. A place where weird is an advantage."

That was the beginning.

Back in Room 211, Mitchell started rethinking the way he saw both his students and himself.

He was finally beginning to believe it: his job wasn't to be the perfect teacher, but the present one.

The one who showed up, even on the days he had nothing left to give.

The one who didn't always get it right but kept coming back anyway.

He turned the forgotten table in the corner of the classroom into a space that felt different. Not for discipline. Not for make-up work. But for creativity. Reflection. Voice. He set out a sketch pad. A few markers. A blank journal. Above it, he taped up a sign that simply read:

What makes you proud?

At first, nothing happened. But by the end of the week, the table began to fill with belonging.

One student scribbled: *I can do a 360 on my skateboard.*

Another wrote: *I've read forty-three books this year.*

Another: *I make awesome grilled cheese sandwiches.*

They weren't bragging.

They were reclaiming their value.

That's when Tammy passed him in the hallway, glanced over, and smiled. "You're seeing them differently now."

"I think I am," Mitchell said. "And maybe for the first time… they're seeing themselves, too."

She nodded. "That's the moment the job starts to make sense."

Mitchell hesitated. "What do we do for the ones who don't believe they're good at anything?"

Tammy didn't miss a beat.

"We believe it for them until they see it too."

That line rewired something in his thought processes.

He went back to the table in the corner with a new goal:

To *reflect* instead of fix.

To *meet* instead of manage.

He didn't ask what was wrong. He asked what they loved. He didn't tell them what they could be. He reminded them of what they already were. And slowly, the table filled.

With stories. With sketches. With journal entries. With trust.

That space became a small spark of something bigger.

By the end of the month, they launched a class blog together: "Voices from the Corner Table." Students submitted stories, drawings, video clips, and even recipes. And they didn't just share what they were proud of.

They began to *own* it.

One Friday afternoon, as students packed up, Camila handed him another folded paper. On the front, it simply said:

Thanks for sitting with us. You're the first teacher who ever wanted to hang out with us.

He read it twice.

Then he added a sticky note to his desk:

Kids remember the teacher who came to their table.

That night, he wrote in his journal:

The table in the corner isn't a place for leftovers. It's a place for beginnings. You don't have to teach brilliance. You just have to make space for it to show up.

And he underlined it twice.

CHAPTER 12

SEEING THE STUDENTS

IT STARTED AT the corner table. Mitchell had shown up, day after day, just to be present. But what came next wasn't just about showing up. It was about finally seeing.

Mitchell used to think he was observant. Back in his engineering days, he could spot a decimal out of place or a structural flaw in a design in seconds. But teaching had shown him a new truth: You can't fix what you refuse to see. And for weeks, he'd been staring at his students without really seeing them.

That started to change.

It wasn't a single moment but a series of small ones.

He noticed how Jasmine always stayed a few minutes after the bell, erasing the whiteboard without being asked.

How Marcus, for all his disruptions, never let another student sit alone.

How Leah, quiet in class, lit up when talking about her dog.

They weren't just names on a roster. They were stories. They were trying. They were bright in ways no standardized test could ever measure.

One afternoon, while sorting papers left on the corner table, Mitchell came across a folded index card. No name. Just a line scribbled in pencil:

"I fix stuff. Like fans, lamps, vacuums… mostly things people throw away."

He flipped it over. A rough diagram of what looked like a motor was sketched on the back, labeled with arrows and notes.

Mitchell blinked.

This wasn't a typical answer to any assignment. But it was something more important. A glimpse of who a student *was*—outside the frame of school.

He stared at it a moment longer, then set it aside gently, almost reverently.

Tammy had told him, "We teach content. But more importantly, we teach students. How a student sees themselves will determine everything else."

He hadn't fully understood that until now.

There's no such thing as a standard student.

Every child has strengths. Every child has brilliance.

But brilliance doesn't always raise its hand. Sometimes it hides in the margins. Sometimes it acts out. Sometimes it stays quiet because it's been ignored before.

Mitchell started changing the way he took attendance. Instead of just calling names, he'd ask a simple question:

"What's something you're good at that school doesn't measure?"

The first time, he got shrugs. Confused looks. One kid asked if it was for a grade.

But then the answers came.

"Fixing bikes." "Cooking." "Writing poems, but I don't like letting people read them." "Helping my brother with his speech homework."

He wrote them down. Every one. Because if he didn't, who would?

That week, he added a new section to the back wall of Room 211: Strength Space. Students could write or draw something they were proud of, something that had nothing to do with school.

Within days, it filled.

Drawings. Notes. Snapshots of self-worth.

One card read: *I can do a backflip. No cap.*

Another: *I made dinner every night this week.*

And then one that stopped him cold:

I help take care of my little sister so my mom can sleep. That's why I'm tired all the time.

He stared at that one the longest, recognizing Jasmine's handwriting.

Suddenly, it all made sense. Jasmine wasn't disengaged. She was exhausted.

The next day, Mitchell looked at his class differently. Not as students to manage, but humans to believe in.

He realized he wasn't teaching future test-takers. He was teaching future chefs, mechanics, parents, artists, friends, leaders. He was shaping how they'd see themselves long after they left Room 211.

That day, before the bell, he wrote on the board:

You don't have to be like everyone else to be great.

As the students came in, several paused.

"Is that for us?" someone asked.

Mitchell smiled. "That's for all of us."

After class, Tammy peeked in. "You're starting to see it, huh?"

"What's that?"

"The difference between teaching students and seeing them."

He nodded. "Every single one of them has something."

Tammy grinned. "They always have. Now you're paying attention."

That night, Mitchell opened his journal and wrote:

When we look for brilliance, we find it. When we believe it's there, students start to believe it too.

He underlined it twice.

Room 211 didn't look all that different, but it had changed—because the teacher had.

He didn't change the lesson plan.

He changed the lens.

One question. One wall. One new way of seeing students for who they already were.

It wasn't a massive leap forward.

It was a one-degree shift.

Small. Intentional. Real.

The kind of shift that doesn't get posted on data walls, but it transforms how you teach forever.

CHAPTER 13

REACH THEM WHERE THEY LIVE

THERE WERE STILL students Mitchell hadn't quite reached yet. Johnny was one of them.

He sat in the back of the room, hoodie up like a knight's helm, eyes half-shut but always tracking. He didn't speak unless spoken to. Didn't disrupt. Didn't engage. Just existed at the edge of things, quiet, closed off, drifting.

Most teachers would've called him unmotivated. Mitchell knew better.

He'd seen the notebook half-filled with sketches and hand-drawn maps, tiny character names written in the margins, pixelated weapons and strategy charts scrawled like blueprints. Johnny wasn't unmotivated. He just hadn't been invited in.

Mitchell remembered what Tammy had been telling him: "You have to reach them before you can teach them." It echoed in his mind as he looked across the classroom at Johnny. So, he decided to try something outside the box.

He posted a flyer on the board: Game Night (Friday after school): Pizza, Games, No homework allowed.

A few students lit up. Johnny didn't say anything. But Mitchell noticed the way his eyes flicked toward the flyer. Twice.

That Friday, kids filtered into the library. Some brought their own consoles. Mitchell helped set up multiple TVs in the corners of the room, each linked to a console, controllers piled on tables, cords taped to the floor. It looked more like a tournament arena than a library, and that was the point. A space where kids could just be kids.

There were sodas, snacks, and enough energy in the room to light up the county. They split into teams. Mitchell, having grown up on games, was still a contender—or at least he thought.

But Johnny? Johnny was next level.

Movement. Timing. Team coordination. Calm under pressure. Within two rounds, everyone wanted Johnny on their squad.

By the end of the night, Johnny wasn't the kid in the back of the room anymore. He was the guy everyone was talking to, high-fiving, and bragging about.

On Monday, Mitchell had hardly stepped into Room 211 before hearing a student say, "Yo, Johnny! What time were you on last night?"

Another added, "You wiped that whole squad by yourself. Total GOAT."

Mitchell didn't say a word. Just watched.

Connection had happened. Not through content. Not through consequence. Through the opportunity for Johnny to finally be himself.

And that's when Mitchell realized something he'd been missing.

Not all relevance is academic. Not all connection has to be tied to a standard.

Sometimes, we have to reach students where they already are, on their turf, in their world. And when we do? We give them something they may have never had at school: a *win*.

That night, Mitchell wrote in his journal:

How many students come to school every day having never experienced success? How many walk through our doors with no confidence in who they are or what they can do?

He let the question sit.

Confidence grows in the soil of success. Just one moment can change everything.

The next morning, he asked Johnny to help set up Chromebooks before class. Johnny was happy to demonstrate his tech skills.

The day after, he handed Johnny the dry-erase marker. "Want to write the assignment on the board for me?"

Johnny wrote the assignment on the board before boldly signing it with his screen name.

Mitchell said nothing. No correction. No praise. Just trust.

And over time, that trust turned into presence. That presence turned into participation. And eventually, Johnny, once invisible, became someone others looked up to.

It reminded Mitchell of something he'd read back in college literature class. *Pygmalion.* The sculptor who carved a statue so lovingly, it came to life.

His professor had explained it this way: People tend to become what we believe about them. If we believe they can grow, they do. If we assume they won't, they rarely try.

It was called *the Pygmalion effect.* And Mitchell could see it playing out before his very eyes.

That night, he sat with his journal open, the words already forming before his pen touched the page.

Believe a student can be great and treat them accordingly, and they'll often rise. Believe they can't, and they'll believe it, too.

He thought back to Johnny in the back row, hood pulled on, invisible to most.

And then to Johnny on game night, center of the room, skills on display, laughter and pride wrapped around him, drawing in others like moths to a flame, replacing the armor he would no longer need.

Reach them where they live, Mitchell wrote. *Because sometimes, the best lessons don't come from the board. They come from showing a kid who they already are.*

That was the real rigor.

Seeing their brilliance and letting them experience it, too.

Because success doesn't just change performance.

It changes identity.

And in Room 211, that was the first standard they aimed to meet.

CHAPTER

14

LOVE WHO YOU TEACH

MONDAY MORNING, JUST before first period, the principal stepped into Room 211, carrying a travel mug and wearing a knowing smile. Mitchell looked up, caught off guard by her timing.

"Just checking in," she said. "Heard game night was a big hit. The kids are still talking about it. And I've seen a change in some of your students. Keep doing what you're doing, Mr. Karns."

He didn't know how to respond.

"Teachers like you do more than just survive," she added. "They build something that lasts."

She gave him a nod and left, just as quickly as she'd come.

As the door closed behind her, Mitchell opened his desk drawer and pulled out his journal. The words he had written earlier leapt off the page:

Love what you teach, but love who you teach more.

He had written it down in the first week, back when he was still trying to fake confidence and outrun the chaos. Back when he didn't fully understand what it meant.

He had reread that note several times since jotting it down. He had liked the idea. But now, after several months of failed lessons, surprising wins, and real connections, he understood it.

Later that morning, Mitchell wrote it on the whiteboard in big, bold letters. Nothing else. No warm-up. No agenda. Just the words.

Students trickled in and paused.

"Who wrote that?" Jasmine asked.

"I did," Mitchell said.

"It sounds like something Ms. Tammy would say."

Mitchell smiled. "It is."

By third period, the quote had added its own kind of energy to the room, unspoken, but present. Like an invitation to breathe.

At lunchtime, Marcus pointed at it as he walked out. "That's kinda corny," he muttered, but his voice didn't have its usual edge. And he was the last one to leave that day, holding the door for two classmates without being asked.

Tammy popped her head into Room 211 that afternoon after knocking twice.

She glanced at the board, then at Mitchell. "You're definitely starting to get it."

He shrugged. "Still working on it."

"I would say you're really living it," she countered, stepping inside.

She looked around the room at the reset zone in the back, at the desks no longer in rows, and at the sticky notes on Mitchell's desk. "You've gone above and beyond. You didn't have to plan game night. You didn't have to learn their quirks. You didn't have to show up the way you have. But you did. That's love."

Mitchell looked at her. "Sometimes I think I'm doing too much."

Tammy raised an eyebrow. "You're doing exactly what kids remember. Most won't remember the formulas. But they'll remember who believed in them when they couldn't believe in themselves."

He nodded.

She continued, "Loving who you teach doesn't mean coddling them.

It means committing to their success, even when they resist it. Especially when they resist it."

Mitchell thought back to Johnny. To Marcus. To the tiny wins that weren't in the pacing guide but meant everything.

Tammy leaned against the desk. "You've created a space where they feel seen. That's rare. It's sacred."

He didn't speak. He didn't have to.

Before she walked out, Tammy added, "Keep that quote up. They need it. But maybe you do too."

After school, Mitchell sat in his chair a while longer than usual. The room was quiet, the kind of quiet that settles not in your ears, but in your bones. The kind that gives space to think.

He thought about the first week. The chaos. The self-doubt. The moments he wanted to run. And now he was truly hearing laughter in the mornings, fielding questions instead of complaints, seeing kids linger after the bell to share a few extra moments with their classmates.

He thought about Jasmine asking for help without sarcasm. About Marcus showing a new student around. About Johnny helping reset chairs after lunch without being asked.

It was working. Maybe not every day. Maybe not perfectly. But it was real.

That night, Mitchell stayed late *because he wanted to.*

He straightened the desks. Wrote notes of encouragement for a few students. Refilled the pencil cup. Cleaned the whiteboard.

Then stood back and stared at the words: *Love what you teach, but love* who *you teach more.*

He thought about Emma and what he hoped her future teachers would be like. Would they love the content more than her? Or would they look past the grades and effort and see the full person?

He thought about himself at twelve—awkward, angry, trying too hard to seem like he didn't care. He wondered who he might've become if someone had loved who he was becoming instead of what he wasn't yet.

As he sat back down at his desk, he pulled out a fresh sticky note and wrote:

They won't remember the math. But they'll remember that I cared about them.

He stuck it next to the others.

As he got up to leave, he dimmed the lights and stood in the doorway.

The room didn't feel like a classroom anymore. It felt like a place that mattered.

CAMILA DOESN'T TALK

MITCHELL SAT AT his desk, trying to make sense of the paperwork that had piled up throughout the week. It had been a chaotic couple of days in Room 211. Students seemed to be particularly restless, and despite his best efforts to manage the classroom, things were slipping through his fingers. His attention kept returning to the quiet corner of the room, where Camila sat at her desk, almost invisible to the others.

Camila was one of those students who barely made a sound in class. She never volunteered to answer questions, never raised her hand. She rarely made eye contact with him, except when he walked by her desk. She sat in the back, always with her head slightly tilted, absorbing everything around her without actively participating. Mitchell had noticed this behavior before, how she quietly watched others, scribbling in a notebook, never once asking for attention.

What was it about her?

At first, Mitchell had assumed that she was just shy. There were plenty of students like that, right? The quiet ones who blended into the background. He tried not to think too much about it. After all, she was doing her work, getting her assignments in on time. But there was something about the way she avoided interacting with anyone, even when others reached out, that bothered him. She never seemed fully engaged, even though her eyes seemed to be constantly observing everything that went on around her.

One day, after class, Mitchell stayed behind to straighten up the room and grade papers. He was organizing the whiteboard markers when he noticed Camila lingering at the back of the room. He had become so used to her silence that he almost didn't notice her at all. But today, there was something different. She wasn't at her desk. Instead, she stood near the back corner, head down, her pencil moving across the paper in steady, rhythmic strokes. Mitchell walked over, curious.

"What are you working on, Camila?" he asked, unsure if she would even respond.

She stopped drawing for a moment, looking up at him. There was a brief moment of hesitation, and then, in a soft voice, she answered, "Just another drawing."

Mitchell looked at her notebook. It wasn't just doodles. It was an intricate sketch of a girl standing beneath a tree, her gaze turned upward as though searching for something in the sky. The drawing wasn't perfect, but it was thoughtful. There was a story in those lines and shading, something far deeper than a casual doodle.

"I really like that one," Mitchell said, impressed by the detail. He wasn't an artist himself, but he could tell that she put extra detail into this piece. "Do you draw a lot?"

Camila nodded, slowly turning the sketchbook around so he could see more. "Sometimes. When I don't know how to say things."

Mitchell's heart sank. *When I don't know how to say things.* The weight of her words hung in the air. He had been so quick to assume that Camila was just disengaged, that she simply didn't care. But in this quiet moment, he realized that he had missed something crucial. Camila wasn't silent because she didn't want to participate. She was silent because she didn't know how to speak. Not in the traditional sense that most teachers expected. But in her own way, she had been speaking all along. Mitchell had just failed to listen as much as he should.

The next few days passed in a blur, but Mitchell couldn't shake the conversation with Camila. Her quiet presence was always in the back of his mind. She was still watching the world, not taking part in it, but now he saw her differently. She wasn't withdrawn. She wasn't ignoring him or the class. She was simply processing the world in her own way.

As the week went on, Mitchell began to observe Camila more closely. He noticed how she interacted with others, not through words, but through small gestures. When another student dropped their pencil, Camila was the first to hand it back. When classmates asked for help with assignments, she would offer a quick note of assistance with a brief smile accompanying her quiet actions.

Her brilliance, Mitchell realized, wasn't in the answers she gave on tests or the assistance she offered others in class. It wasn't in a loud voice or confident hand raised in the air. Her brilliance was in the way she showed up, every day, in the subtle moments that went unnoticed by most. It was in the way she spoke through her art, in the way she was present even when she didn't say a word.

That afternoon, Mitchell stayed late again. He was fine-tuning tomorrow's lesson when Tammy knocked twice on the doorframe and stepped in. Her eyes swept the room—noticing the updated seating chart, a small display labeled *Strength Space*, and the handwritten notes now taped along the back wall.

"Looks like Room 211's getting a little soul," she said, smiling.

Mitchell gave a tired smile. "I'm hoping so. Still feels like I'm not breaking through with some of them, though. Camila, for one—she's so quiet, and I can't tell if I'm reaching her at all."

Tammy walked over, leaning against the desk. "Mitchell, it's easy to focus on the kids who are loudest, the ones who seek attention. But there are always others who have something to say. They just don't do it the way we expect. Camila is likely silent because that's how she communicates. And if you're patient enough, you'll see the brilliance in the silence."

Mitchell looked at Tammy, considering her words. She continued,

"We spend so much time looking for the obvious signs of engagement, the raised hands, the loud voices. But there's more happening than just that. The students who don't speak up, like Camila, can teach us a lot if we let them."

One afternoon, Mitchell sat at his desk reviewing some lesson plans when Camila's soft voice broke through his thoughts. She was standing in front of him, clutching her sketchbook.

"Mr. Karns," she said, her voice barely above a whisper. "Would you like to see another one?"

He looked up and smiled. "Of course. Let's see."

She opened the sketchbook to reveal a drawing of a small group of students, sitting together, laughing. At first glance, it seemed simple, but the warmth in the way the figures were drawn, their postures, the expressions on their faces, held a subtle complexity.

"It's us," Camila said, almost shyly. "The class."

Mitchell's eyes softened as he took in the drawing. The visuals extended far beyond just depicting a group of kids on paper; it was a moment frozen in time. Her classmates, the laughter they shared, the connections they made, all of it captured in the lines and shadows of her art. Mitchell realized that Camila had given him more than just a drawing; it was an invitation to see the world through her eyes.

"This is beautiful," he said, his voice thick with emotion. "You've captured something really special."

Camila gave a small nod, but her eyes glowed with something more than just approval. There was pride in the way she looked at him. She wasn't used to being noticed for the things she did differently, but now, for the first time, someone had seen her silent brilliance.

As the weeks passed, Mitchell made a conscious effort to pay attention to those who, like Camila, communicated in ways that weren't always visible. In each of them, Mitchell began to recognize the power of patience and observation. Some students, like Camila, didn't speak out loud. But that didn't mean they didn't have something important to say. Teachers just had to be patient enough to listen and creative enough to look beyond words.

The next time Mitchell had a lesson where students were encouraged to share their thoughts out loud, he made sure to carve out space for Camila. He didn't push her to speak; he didn't demand that she participate the way others did. Instead, he invited her to share, through her art or through whatever medium felt most comfortable. And when she did speak, however softly, it was clear that she always had something of great value to offer.

Mitchell realized:

Some students speak in silence.

Be the teacher who hears them too.

CHAPTER
16

GIVE ME A BREAK

It was 1:45 p.m. on a Friday, and Room 211 was running on fumes.

Mitchell glanced around the classroom. Jasmine had her head resting on her open textbook, her pen moving lazily across the page. Marcus spun his water bottle like it was the only thing keeping him awake. A few kids stared at the clock like they could will it forward.

Earlier in the year, Mitchell would have seen the mood as defiant, but not recognized it for what it was: *depletion.*

Mitchell could feel it in himself, too, that low-battery hum behind the eyes. The kind of tired that coffee couldn't quench. He flipped through his lesson plans and knew immediately: No one had the bandwidth for what he had planned. Not them. Not him.

He could push through, force the review activity, collect the exit tickets, and drag everyone across the finish line with a combination of forced enthusiasm and sheer willpower.

But why?

For what?

He leaned back in his chair and let the silence stretch. It wasn't rebellious. It was honest. The room felt heavy, like it was holding its breath, waiting for something to change.

He looked around again. The kids were drained, but it wasn't just physical tiredness. It was the kind of exhaustion that comes from trying to be something you're not, trying to perform every minute of every day, constantly meeting expectations that no one had ever stopped to question.

Then it hit him.

Maybe today wasn't about delivering content, checking boxes, or pushing students to meet academic standards. Maybe it was about *letting them breathe*.

Mitchell stood up, stretching his back and looking at the clock. He watched it tick a few more seconds, then he walked to the front of the class and wiped the objective off the whiteboard.

"Alright. Close your notebooks."

Several heads lifted, confused. A couple of students glanced around at each other fearing a pop quiz or other academic torture.

"We're not doing the lesson," Mitchell said. "Pack up. We're going outside."

Jasmine blinked. "Wait, for real?"

Marcus sat up straighter. "No cap?"

Mitchell smiled. "Dead serious. We need a brain boost."

They looked at each other like he'd just offered them an extra recess.

He didn't wait for applause. Just walked to the door and held it open.

Out in the fresh air, the class came back to life. The sun was warm but not hot. A breeze carried the scent of cut grass and late spring. The playground was mostly empty, the fields wide open. It felt like possibility.

Jasmine did a cartwheel.

Marcus ran a full sprint across the field for no reason other than he could.

Mitchell stood at the edge of the grass, watching. No clipboards. No timers. No rubric.

He felt his own tension start to melt away as he watched his students. They weren't learning through tasks but simply being themselves. The joy of movement, the laughter, and the camaraderie that formed in the moments where they were allowed to just *play* reminded him that learning didn't always have to be about structured activities or rigid expectations. Sometimes it was about giving students a space to feel *human*.

Mitchell remembered his own childhood, how recess was more than just a break. It was where he recharged. It was where he built bonds with friends, where he found joy in the simplest things, like kicking a ball or running across a field without thinking about tests or grades.

Play wasn't wasted time. It was essential.

He grabbed a football from the PE bin and tossed it toward a group of students. Within minutes, a game broke out, some playing, others watching and cheering. There was laughter, competition, and the kind of joy that didn't need structure. For the first time that day, Mitchell saw them *engaged* in something that made them feel alive.

He saw kids connecting in ways they never did inside four walls. Marcus high-fived someone he usually ignored. Jasmine cheered for a classmate who often sat alone. Even the quiet kids laughed out loud.

That's when Tammy appeared, clipboard in hand, clearly on her way back from a meeting. She stopped, squinting across the field.

"You skipping class, Mr. Karns?" she called.

Mitchell grinned. "Absolutely."

Tammy walked over and stood beside him, watching the chaos with a knowing look.

"You know my motto," she said.

Mitchell nodded. "Work hard, play hard."

"More than a slogan," she said. "It's survival."

She looked out at the students laughing, moving, recharging in ways no standardized curriculum could quantify.

"It's funny," she continued, "how we expect kids to show up, sit still, push through, and work hard all day without joy, without breaks, without laughter. But adults? We build fun into everything.

"Look at fitness centers. You think there are TVs on every treadmill because people love cardio? No, we know that if it isn't enjoyable, people won't stick with it. We always dangle the proverbial carrot for adults—rewards, perks, little escapes. But somehow, we act like school should be the one place where fun is off-limits."

Mitchell raised an eyebrow. "So… learning should be entertaining?"

"Well," she said. "Sometimes it can be. But it should at least be engaging. It should be human. Kids love to laugh. They love to play. Why would we separate that from learning when it's the very thing that opens them up to it?"

In that moment, Mitchell wasn't just witnessing a classroom management strategy. He was watching a mindset. One that treated fun not as a distraction from learning but as a doorway into it.

Back in Room 211, the vibe had shifted. The kids weren't bouncing off the walls. They seemed centered. Grounded. The edge had worn off.

Mitchell didn't say much. Just wrote one sentence on the board:

Sometimes the best way to reset the mind is to move the body. And maybe even have a little fun while you're at it.

No one questioned it.

Many of them smiled.

They got it.

He looked around at his class. They were people with stories, with weights on their shoulders, with a need for moments that weren't about performance or grades.

Later, at his desk, Mitchell opened his notebook and jotted down a reminder:

Tired minds don't need more pressure. They need permission to breathe.

Then another line came to him, one that felt like it had been waiting to be written:

Classrooms shouldn't feel like pressure cookers. They should feel like places to grow.

He stared at those lines for a while, the silence in the room wrapping around him like a new kind of comfort.

He thought about what Tammy had said, how teaching burns off your illusions until only the truth remains. The truth was, he didn't have all the answers. But he had something to give.

The next morning, he walked into Room 211 with less weight on his shoulders and more purpose in his step.

And for the first time, he felt like he belonged in that building.

Teaching, after all, wasn't about knowing everything.

It was about knowing why you're there.

CHAPTER 17

EMBRACING SETBACKS

MITCHELL WAS AT his desk again, staring at yet another stack of papers in front of him. Another day. Another lesson that fell flat. The students were distracted, another tough day, and no matter what he tried, he couldn't seem to get them to engage.

The kind of day that makes even passionate teachers question everything. He exhaled hard.

The bell rang; students filed out, backpacks dragging, laughter echoing in the hallway. Mitchell stayed seated, his eyes on a single paper where a student had answered five questions—not with words, but with hand-drawn memes.

Some were funny.

One actually made him laugh.

But none of them answered the questions.

He sighed, leaned back, and picked up his phone. Scrolled mindlessly through social media, half-zoned out until a certain post stopped him cold:

If you don't enjoy spending time around children, you're in the wrong profession.

He read it twice.

He looked around the empty room, the crumpled papers on the floor, the pencil that had been chewed beyond recognition, the crooked poster that read "Mistakes Are Proof You're Trying."

Then he stood, walked to the board, and in quiet, clean strokes wrote:

If you don't enjoy spending time around children, you're in the wrong profession.

It hit him harder than he expected.

He was here to do more than teach. He was here to be present. To show up for these kids, even on days when they didn't want it and especially on days when he didn't want to.

Just as he was packing his things, he heard the telltale knocks on his door.

"That's a good one," Tammy said, nodding at the quote. "Where'd you get it?"

"Social media," Mitchell said with a sheepish smile. "Weird how the simplest things land the hardest."

Tammy leaned against the doorframe, arms crossed. "You'll never make it if you don't love the kids. Loving the content is great. Being organized is necessary. But this job demands heart. No amount of training prepares you for the emotional weight."

Mitchell nodded slowly.

"Even when you've come a long way, you'll still have days where nothing lands," she said gently. "Not because you're failing—but because that's the work. Even veteran teachers have those days. What matters is how you carry yourself through them. That's what defines you."

The next morning, Mitchell wrote a new quote at the top of the board before students arrived.

Failure is a , (comma), not a . (period)

As the class settled in, he stood in front of them purposefully.

"I want to talk about failure," he said simply.

That word landed with a thud. A few students froze. A few rolled their eyes. But he kept going.

"Failure isn't something to avoid. It's something to understand. It's how we grow. It's where we learn what we're capable of."

Jasmine raised her hand. "Isn't failure… bad?"

Mitchell shook his head. "Only if we stop there."

He walked over to the board, underlining the quote twice. "This job, my job, isn't about getting you to memorize formulas or ace tests. It's about helping you learn how to keep going when things don't come easy. Life isn't about getting everything right. It's about learning from what goes wrong."

The room was quiet. Present. Listening.

"You don't have to be perfect," he added. "You just have to keep trying."

Over the next few weeks, he noticed another shift in motion.

Sarah, who always hesitated before speaking, started offering answers, even when she wasn't sure. Marcus asked to redo a quiz. Johnny stayed after school for help without being asked.

They weren't afraid of being wrong anymore.

They were learning how to handle setbacks.

And so was Mitchell.

He stopped marking every wrong answer with red ink. Started writing notes instead—"Great thinking here," *"Almost got it—try again."* *"This part makes sense. Build on it." (Or split entirely)* When Jasmine froze during a quiz, he let her finish it later, no questions asked. When Marcus turned in a half-finished assignment, Mitchell didn't scold—he pulled up a chair and asked what had gotten in the way. He was still teaching equations. But more than that, he was teaching recovery, reflection, and the courage to try again.

One afternoon, Mitchell jotted a new note in his journal:

They won't remember the worksheets. But they might remember who helped them get back up.

This chapter of his journey didn't end in applause. There were no grand breakthroughs. Just small yet significant ones.

A raised hand.

A second try.

A shy "Can I get help with this?"

And Mitchell realized:

Some students just need a chance.

Others may need a second, a third, or even a fourth.

Either way, they need a teacher who doesn't give up on them.

THE POWER OF YET

WEDNESDAY SETTLED OVER Room 211 like a fog—quiet, thick, and hard to shake. It wasn't noise or chaos that wore Mitchell down this time. It was the quiet. The slump in shoulders. The restless tapping of pencils. The way even the lights seemed dimmer.

He was halfway through explaining fractions when he saw it: more checked-out eyes than usual, doodles instead of notes, the unspoken weight of disengagement hanging heavy in the air.

He capped the marker and turned to the class.

"Can I ask you something?" he said, setting the marker down.

A few heads lifted.

"Do you hate math?"

A couple of hands shot up. Some smirked. Jasmine didn't even look up, just muttered, "Obviously."

Mitchell chuckled. "Fair. But let me ask a better question."

He walked slowly across the front of the room.

"Do you hate learning?"

This time, Marcus tilted his head. A few students frowned. Jasmine looked up.

"You see," Mitchell said, "I don't think you hate learning. I think you hate feeling like you're bad at it."

Silence. The kind that means something just landed.

"You don't hate math when you figure out how much money you've got to buy snacks, right? Or when you're checking how much change you should've gotten back. You don't hate numbers when you're saving for shoes or a new game."

He paused.

"What you hate is the feeling of being behind. The feeling like everyone else gets it but you. Like you're already losing before you've even started."

Jasmine crossed her arms. "It's like that all the time."

Mitchell nodded. "Yeah. I've felt it too. In seventh grade, I bombed a history project so bad my teacher told me maybe I wasn't an 'academic kid.' I believed her. For a while, I gave up trying. Until one day, someone told me the only thing I was missing was one word: *yet*."

He grabbed a marker and wrote on the board in big letters: *THE POWER OF YET.*

"You don't know it... *yet*. You're not confident in it... *yet*. You're not where you want to be... *yet*. That word changes everything."

Jasmine raised her hand. "But what if you've been trying, and you still don't get it?"

"Then you're closer than you think," Mitchell said. "Growth isn't loud. It's quiet. Invisible, even. But it's happening."

He looked across the room.

"Let me say this: Struggling is a sign of learning. If you don't feel stuck sometimes, you're not stretching."

A few students sat up straighter.

Mitchell smiled. "Look, I know school hasn't always felt like a safe place to mess up. But I want this room to be different. I want it to be a place where it's okay to say, 'I don't get it... yet.' Because *yet* means you haven't given up."

He paused. "Actually... My first week here, I visited Ms. Tammy's class. And you know she has that tradition—before you can walk in, you have to answer a question. Well, I didn't really know the answer, so I just said what I *thought* it might be."

The class chuckled.

He grinned. "Later, she told me that was her favorite answer. She said sometimes, *close enough is enough.*"

Just then, Tammy peeked her head in the door, as if on cue.

Mitchell nodded toward her. "I was just telling them about the time I answered your door question and embarrassed myself.'"

Tammy smiled. "Still my favorite answer."

And with that, she knocked the doorframe twice and continued on toward the break room, just passing through, but somehow always at the right moment.

Mitchell turned back to the class.

"We need to start thinking of struggle like a gym for your brain. It's where strength is built. And every time you keep going, even when it's hard, you're getting stronger."

He wrote one more line under *THE POWER OF YET*:

SAFE STRUGGLE.

"This classroom is a place where struggle is safe. Where you're allowed to ask, mess up, and figure things out. You're not expected to know everything. You're expected to try."

The bell rang, but no one bolted for the door.

Instead, a few students stayed back. Marcus lingered, running a finger along the edge of the whiteboard.

"You really think I can get better at this?" he asked.

Mitchell didn't hesitate. "I don't just think. I know. Because I already see it."

Marcus gave a half-smile. "Not there yet, though."

Mitchell smiled back. "Exactly."

That evening, Mitchell sat in his empty classroom, staring at the words still written on the board. He didn't erase them.

He left them there for tomorrow.

Because tomorrow, someone else might need to see them. Someone else might be feeling like they'll never get it.

And that one, simple word *yet* might change everything.

CHAPTER 19

STEP-UP NIGHT

It was 6:22 p.m. and Mitchell was bustling around Room 211, straightening desks that were already straight, rechecking slides he wouldn't end up using, and sipping his third cup of lukewarm coffee.

Tonight was "Step-Up Night"—a spring event where incoming students and their families visited the school to meet teachers and get a feel for middle school. He glanced at the clock again.

Three families had stopped by so far. Two smiled politely, one asked where the math teacher was, and all three left within five minutes. The room felt like a waiting room without a queue.

From the hallway, he could hear voices. Not loud but energized. Laughter. Applause?

He stepped out and glanced up and down the hall.

Room 212 was full. Tammy's room.

The door was propped open. Inside, parents were moving, talking, smiling. One was writing on a whiteboard. Another was pretending to be a student, laughing as Tammy handed out mini whiteboards and dry-erase markers.

Mitchell stood just outside, unsure whether to keep watching or retreat.

Tammy noticed him instantly. She didn't miss much.

She didn't interrupt her captivating parent lesson, but acknowledged him with a subtle smile.

But he had seen everything he needed to.

Back in the oppressive silence of his own room, Mitchell sat on the edge of his desk, looking at the stack of handouts he had printed. They were methodical. Informative. Bullet-pointed to death.

But they didn't say anything real.

Ten minutes later, Tammy stepped in with her usual coffee mug, this time filled with sparkling water.

"You spying on me again?" she said lightly.

"Something like that," Mitchell admitted.

She looked around Room 211. "You had some traffic?"

"A little," he said. "Mostly parents looking for another classroom."

She raised an eyebrow. "And?"

"I don't know," he said. "I thought I did everything right. I had slides. I had a whole outline. But it felt like... like I was trying to host a seminar in a funeral parlor."

Tammy smirked. "Because you forgot the one thing that makes this job work."

He looked at her.

"Connection," she said.

"You even connect with the families," he said. "How do you do that?"

"I treat them like I treat the kids. With respect. With curiosity. And with the belief that they're part of the team."

Mitchell rubbed his forehead. "I feel like I missed the mark."

Tammy shook her head. "You just aimed too low. You were trying to inform. That's fine. But if you want them on your side, you've got to involve them. Let them feel what learning looks like. Let them experience what it's like to be in your room."

He nodded slowly.

"You're doing good work," she added. "But don't be afraid to let people see who you are. That's the teacher they'll remember. That's the one their kids talk about at dinner."

She turned to go, but paused at the door.

"Oh, and next time? No PowerPoint. Make them laugh. Make them think. Maybe even make them solve a math problem together."

He raised an eyebrow.

"Trust me," she said. "A little discomfort makes people remember how hard it is to be a student. It builds empathy. And empathy builds bridges."

He sat there for a long while after she left.

Later, as he packed up, Mitchell tore the slides out of the binder and dropped them into the recycling bin.

He grabbed a sticky note and scribbled something in big, uneven letters:

Families need to feel welcomed, too.

He stuck it on the edge of his desk.

Step up night hadn't gone the way he imagined, but the lesson had landed.

Next time, they wouldn't just meet Mr. Karns, the teacher.

They'd meet the one who knew how to connect.

DATA INFORMS.
RELATIONSHIPS
TRANSFORM.

THE SCHOOL WAS buzzing with talk about test prep. Emails were flying. Admin walk-throughs were increasing. Charts and color-coded spreadsheets plastered the conference room walls, each one tracking which students were "on the bubble," "below grade level," or "in urgent need of intervention."

Mitchell stared at his inbox, the subject lines blurring together:

ACTION NEEDED: Benchmark Data Review

Reminder: Testing Strategy Meeting Today

FSA Prep Schedule Update

He closed the laptop with a sigh. It wasn't that he didn't want valuable data. He did. He'd spent years in engineering interpreting spreadsheets, mapping progress, and drawing conclusions from numbers. But this felt different. In the corporate world, data pointed to systems. Here, it pointed to students. And the way it was being used felt sterile, like students were just data points on someone else's accountability chart.

Mitchell stared out the window, wondering how many of his students were being reduced to red or yellow zones on a spreadsheet right now, labeled for what they hadn't done, without anyone asking why.

A familiar voice radiated from the doorway.

"You look like you're drowning in acronyms," Tammy said, holding a mug that read *Teaching is a Work of Heart.*

Mitchell gave a tired smile. "Trying to figure out how to get my kids excited about a test that won't tell me anything I don't already know."

She stepped into the room without asking, pulled up a chair, and set a folder on his desk.

"What's this?" he asked.

"My version of data. You may be familiar with some of these."

He opened it. Inside were index cards, one for every student. But instead of scores, there were notes.

> *Johnny—Loves video games. Great at problem-solving when it's tied to real-world stuff.*
>
> *Jasmine—Strong writer. Gets anxious with timed tests. Needs to know you see her.*
>
> *Marcus—Quick thinker. Sarcastic when he's insecure. Loves being a helper. Invite him to lead more.*

Mitchell flipped through the cards slowly, reading them like sacred text.

"You keep all this?"

"Of course," Tammy said. "It's the only data that helps me teach."

He looked up. "But admin wants charts and benchmarks and growth goals."

Tammy shrugged. "And I give them that. But this," she tapped the folder, "is what actually changes outcomes."

Mitchell exhaled. "I've been feeling like I'm behind because I'm not diving deep into the latest testing standards."

She raised an eyebrow. "Don't confuse data with insight. And don't confuse performance with potential. You know your students better than any test ever will."

She stood now, pacing a bit, animated, locked in.

"In fact, as a whole group, we, the teachers, know these kids better than anyone. That's why it's so important to know them. Their strengths. Where they struggle. What they're passionate about. We're not educating a brain, Mitchell. We're educating a child."

Mitchell nodded slowly, her words settling in deeper than he expected.

"They keep asking for more rigor," he said. "But how can we bring out their best if we don't even know them?"

"Exactly," Tammy said. "We're told to close the achievement gap. But you can't close a gap if you're blind to what a kid is carrying."

She pointed to a sticky note on his monitor.

"You wrote, 'Be the person they need.' Right? Well, they don't need someone who treats them like a test score. They need someone who sees the story behind the score. Who knows when they're falling apart and when they're ready to shine."

Mitchell glanced back at the folder. "So you track their stories?"

She nodded. "Stories are data, too. They just don't fit in a spreadsheet."

There was a pause. Then Tammy added something that stopped him cold.

"I've never seen a test score transform a student. But I've seen great teachers do it again and again."

Mitchell didn't respond.

He just reached into his desk, pulled out a fresh stack of index cards, and started writing names.

Mitchell didn't respond. He just reached into his desk, pulled out a fresh stack of index cards, and started writing names.

Before she walked out, she turned back. "Standardized tests measure performance on one, specific day. Your classroom? It measures what kind of adults they're becoming every day."

The door clicked shut behind her.

Mitchell sat for a while longer, thumbing through the cards she left him. He looked around Room 211, imagining the kids who sat in those desks. Their jokes. Their outbursts. Their questions. Their quiet courage.

Then he picked up a marker and wrote on the corner of the board:

Data informs. Relationships transform.

That was the standard he would teach by.

Not because it was required.

But because it was human.

CHAPTER 21

FIRE DRILL WISDOM

THE FIRE ALARM blared just as Mitchell was handing out the warm-up.

A shrill, piercing blast, three seconds long, then a pause. Then again. It was clearly a drill. But logic and routine don't mean much when you're dealing with middle schoolers on a Wednesday afternoon.

"Grab your coats!" someone shouted, even though it was nearly eighty degrees outside.

"No, it's not cold, don't worry about it," another yelled, already halfway out the door.

Mitchell raised his voice. "Okay, guys, single file. Let's go. Walk. Don't run."

But the tide was already rushing out. Backpacks thumped. Chairs scraped. Someone tried to take their laptop. One student shouted that it was a real fire, which sent three more into a panicked sprint. A kid ducked back into the room to retrieve their hoodie. Another tried to FaceTime his mom "just in case."

Mitchell's nerves frayed with every clumsy, chaotic step toward the exit.

He did his best to usher them through the congested hallways, navigating a traffic jam of students and staff. It felt like trying to herd a colony of maniacal cats.

And then, when they finally spilled onto the back field, he saw the class from Room 212.

Tammy's class was already there.

They stood in a calm arc. Some were chatting quietly. A few were sitting on the grass. No one was shouting, running, or trying to turn the moment into a spectacle. While not exactly silent, they were settled. Grounded.

Tammy stood off to the side, sipping her coffee like she had all the time in the world. She wasn't directing them with loud commands. She wasn't patrolling them like a drill sergeant. She was just present, watching, scanning, and anchoring their energy.

Her students weren't behaving because of fear. They were following because they trusted her.

Mitchell took a deep breath and turned to his own class, who were still buzzing like bees in a jar. He counted heads, called names, and tried to restore a sliver of order. But the contrast was hard to ignore.

He looked across the field again at Tammy's class, shining examples of tranquility in the chaos. And he wondered, not for the first time, what it would take to get there.

When the drill ended and everyone filed back into the building, Mitchell returned to Room 211 and began picking up the scattered remains of the warm-up that never happened. Half the worksheets were still on desks. One had been trampled in the hallway. The remainder of class was difficult, but they managed to cover at least part of the lesson before dismissal.

Just as he was about to sit down, Tammy stepped into the doorway with her standard double knock.

"That was... something," Mitchell said, running a hand through his hair.

Tammy smiled. "You survived."

"Barely," he muttered.

She leaned against the doorframe, mug still in hand. "You know why we do these drills, right?"

Mitchell raised an eyebrow. "Because the district says we have to?"

She smirked. "Not exactly. We do them because we want their reaction to be calm even when the environment isn't. The alarm isn't the problem. Our reaction is."

He nodded slowly, still catching his breath.

"Your kids handled it like pros," he said. "I mean it. They were just... solid."

Tammy shrugged. "That didn't happen overnight."

Mitchell tilted his head. "So, what is it? What's the secret?"

"No secret. Just practice. Patience. And a whole lot of modeling."

She stepped inside now, lowering her voice. "I wasn't always like this, you know. My first fire drill? Disaster. Total panic. I yelled the whole time. Nearly half the class cried. One kid climbed under a desk and refused to come out. It was bad."

Mitchell blinked. "Seriously?"

"Oh yeah," she said. "Afterward, my mentor pulled me aside and said something I'll never forget: 'They're kids. They don't need your panic. They need your peace. Structure, patience, and for you to keep your cool, especially when everything else is going sideways.'"

She tapped her mug thoughtfully. "That changed everything for me."

Mitchell sank onto the edge of his desk. "So, it's not about being in control. It's about being consistent."

Tammy nodded. "Exactly. You can't fake calm. And if you don't bring it, they'll borrow their energy from the loudest person in the room, and oftentimes, that's the wrong one."

He exhaled. "I keep thinking if I nail the lesson plan, the behavior will follow."

She shook her head. "A perfect lesson doesn't matter if the classroom isn't ready for it. It's like trying to light a candle in a windstorm—it won't catch."

She glanced around his room, desks askew, papers still out of place. Then back at him.

"Teaching isn't just content delivery. It's emotional leadership. When things get loud, when the system shakes, when the fire alarm goes off, literally or not, they're watching you to decide how safe they feel."

Mitchell sat with that for a minute. He looked down at the warm-up he never got to finish.

"They were really shaken," he said.

"And they will be again," Tammy said. "Because life is full of fire drills. Full of moments that feel bigger than they are. Our job is to be the calm in the chaos. Every time."

She turned to go, then paused.

"They won't remember what you were teaching when the alarm went off. But they'll remember what it felt like to be in your presence when it did."

After she left, Mitchell took out his sticky notes.

He picked up a pen and wrote five simple words:

Be the calm in the chaos.

He stayed there, reading them again and again, letting them sink in.

The best teachers don't just teach the lesson.

They lead through the noise. They breathe when others shout. They show students, by example, that it's possible to stay grounded even when the alarms are blaring.

And that, more than any lesson plan, is what makes a classroom feel like home.

CHAPTER

22

YOU DON'T NEED A TITLE TO LEAD

THE LAST BELL had already rung. The hallway buzz was fading. Most teachers had packed up and headed home. But not Mitchell. He was sitting at his desk, grading quizzes and half-listening to the muffled sound of chairs scraping floors and doors slamming shut.

Knock. Knock.

Tammy walked in, as always, holding a half-empty coffee mug and a folder tucked under her arm. "You know," she said, "you stay late enough and they're going to start asking you to lock up."

He smiled. "I don't mind. The quiet helps me think."

She looked around the room, then sat down in one of the student desks. "Thinking's good. So long as it doesn't turn into second-guessing."

Mitchell didn't answer.

Tammy nodded, reading his silence. "I've seen that look before. You're wondering if you're doing enough."

He sighed. "I just… I see how students respond to you. They respect you. Trust you. I keep thinking maybe I'll get there. But it's like I'm waiting for some title or badge to make it feel real."

Tammy leaned forward. "Let me tell you something. I've never wanted a title. I never chased one. I've never needed it."

Mitchell raised an eyebrow. "Then how did you end up with this kind of influence?"

She smiled. "Because leadership isn't about position. It's about presence."

He didn't respond. She kept going.

"You want to know the truth?" she said. "I used to say yes to everything. Stayed late. Picked up extra duties. Took on other people's stress like it was my job. I thought being a good teacher meant being selfless to the point of exhaustion. That if I didn't pour everything into everyone else, I wasn't doing it right."

Mitchell looked up. "So what changed?"

"My body. My spirit. My relationships," she said. "I burned out."

She looked away for a second. "I gave so much I had nothing left. And guess what? The system didn't stop to refill me. It just kept asking for more."

Mitchell nodded slowly. "I feel that."

Tammy continued, her voice firmer now. "That's when I learned something no one told me in teacher prep: You cannot sustain leadership without boundaries. You can't lead from depletion."

She took a breath. "So, I set my priorities and started being more assertive. Not aggressive. Not cold. But clear. I started saying no. I stopped apologizing for needing time, space, or support. And the irony? That's when people started to respect me more."

Mitchell leaned in. "Because you weren't stretched thin?"

"Because I wasn't scared to be honest," she said. "Because I stopped over-explaining and started protecting my energy. Assertiveness isn't about being loud. It's about being grounded. It's about knowing your value and communicating it without guilt."

She sat up straighter. "You don't need a title to lead, Mitchell. But you do need to lead yourself. If you don't set the standard for how people treat you, the job will. And it's not kind."

Mitchell thought for a moment. "That's hard for teachers. We're wired to serve."

"Exactly," Tammy said. "But service without boundaries becomes martyrdom. And we don't need martyrs. We need models. We need teachers who show students what it looks like to speak up respectfully, to set limits without guilt, and to say yes to what matters."

She reached into her folder and pulled out a small laminated card.

"This," she said, "is something I share with first-year teachers."

On the card was written:

- *You can't be everything to everyone.*
- *Boundaries aren't barriers. They're bridges to longevity.*
- *Saying* no *to one thing means saying* yes *to your priorities.*
- *Your time and energy are limited. Guard them like gold.*
- *The most respected leaders don't do it all. They know what not to do.*

Mitchell read it twice.

She added, "You don't need to raise your voice to lead. You need to raise your standards for yourself, for your time, for your classroom. That's how you create impact without burning out."

He looked up. "That's in your book, isn't it?"

Tammy grinned. "Page 212 of my future memoir."

He laughed. "Let me know when it hits shelves." They laughed.

Tammy stood to leave. "Leadership starts when you realize your voice matters and stop waiting for permission to use it."

As she walked down the hallway, Mitchell stared at the card.

He thought about the students who watched his every move, even when they acted like they didn't care. He thought about how many times he had sacrificed lunch, planning periods, even sleep, for everyone else.

He pulled out a sticky note and wrote:

Lead from presence, not position.

And below that:

Protect your energy. The kids are watching.

He smiled, stuck it on his desk, and turned out the light. He didn't need a title.

He was already leading.

CHAPTER

23

THE POWER OF
SMALL WINS

AFTER SCHOOL ON Friday, Mitchell returned to his desk and found a small stack of sticky notes clipped together. No envelope. No explanation. Just Tammy's blocky handwriting on the top one:

Progress is built, not found.

He peeled the clip off and slowly flipped through the stack. Each note had something scribbled on it: quotes, phrases, reminders. Tammy's voice, in ink.

Never underestimate what consistency can build.

Don't chase perfection. Chase presence.

Notice who's never noticed.

He paused at that one.

He remembered Johnny, sitting in the back in that first week of school, invisible and indifferent. He remembered Jasmine, arms crossed, daring him to try. He thought of Marcus, of Camila, of the reset zone, of game night. None of those changes came from some magic formula.

They all came from small, intentional wins.

Tammy had told him once, "You don't get to the summit by jumping. You climb."

Over the course of the year, he had come to understand.

Mitchell had spent so much time early on trying to create the *big moment*. The powerful lesson. The breakthrough day. But it wasn't the grand gestures that changed things, it was the daily routine. The rhythm. The choices that seemed small, but repeated, created something unstoppable.

One sticky note read:

Celebrate the walk, not just the run.

He smiled. He could hear Tammy saying it.

She had always celebrated with her students. Not in a fake, everyone-gets-a-trophy kind of way, but in a real, thoughtful way. When a student who usually didn't speak finally raised her hand, she noticed. When a kid turned in homework for the first time in weeks, she made eye contact and said, "That matters." She celebrated effort because she understood something most teachers missed:

Confidence is built from success. But it's also built from recognition.

Babies don't get trophies for learning to walk, but we cheer anyway. We clap for the first step. The wobble. The fall. Because deep down, we know what it took.

Why should it be any different in the classroom?

Mitchell glanced around Room 211. On the wall near the reset zone, he saw the little jar of notes students had started writing to each other: *Thanks for helping me. You explained that so clearly. You made me laugh today.*

Tiny moments. Big impact.

He walked to the whiteboard and picked up a marker. In bold letters, he wrote:

Small wins are the seeds of greatness.

And below it:

Celebrate what you want to see more of.

That afternoon, Tammy popped her head in.

"No letter," he said.

She shrugged. "Didn't need one."

He held up the sticky notes. "This is better."

Tammy smiled. "The big moments get the attention. The small ones do the changing."

He nodded. "I used to think I had to inspire them."

"And now?"

"I just have to see them. Believe in them. And celebrate the parts they don't even notice in themselves."

She leaned against the doorway. "Exactly. You want to build brilliance in a student? Show them what's already there."

He looked down at the sticky notes. "It's wild. I was chasing breakthroughs. Turns out, they were happening the whole time."

Tammy tapped the doorframe. "Brick by brick."

As she turned to leave, he called after her. "Tammy?"

She looked back.

"Thank you."

Her smile was soft. "It wasn't me, Karns. You just finally slowed down enough to see it."

CHAPTER
24

HELP THEM FIND
THEIR BRILLIANCE

MITCHELL STOOD AT the back of the room, arms crossed, watching his students work on their end-of-term presentations. Not a single slide deck. No rubrics. No grades today. Just voice, creativity, and ownership.

He had asked one simple question:

"What's something you're good at, and how can you use it to help others?"

Some made posters. Some built models. One student wrote a rap. Another taught the class how to stretch when they're stressed. Jasmine gave a tutorial on organizing your binder. Half the class asked for a copy.

Johnny stood up and showed his coding project. A simple game. Nothing flashy. But his face lit up as he explained the logic behind it. Mitchell swore he saw a version of the boy who might someday build something extraordinary.

As the last student sat down, the room fell into a rare kind of stillness. Not silence. But meaning. Presence.

Tammy slipped in unnoticed, this time without even a single knock, leaning in the doorway like she so often did. When the class was dismissed, she stepped forward, watching them file out with quiet pride.

"That," she said, "was a masterclass."

Mitchell laughed, rubbing the back of his neck. "I just got out of the way."

Tammy looked at him. "Exactly."

She walked to the whiteboard and picked up a marker.

EDUCERE, she wrote.

Then, underneath: *To lead out. To bring forth.*

"This is the root of the word *education*," she said. "It's not about cramming in standards. It's about drawing out brilliance. Their strengths. Their voice. Their value."

Mitchell nodded, watching the letters settle like truth.

"You know what we get wrong in this profession?" Tammy continued. "We spend so much time remediating weaknesses that we forget to recognize what kids already do well. And if they never get to see themselves as strong, they stop believing they can ever be."

He exhaled. "I used to think my job was to fill gaps."

"It's not," she said gently. "Your job is to help them see they're not broken. That they have immense value."

She walked to the bulletin board where student work hung, some crooked, some messy, all honest.

Mitchell smiled. "I asked them what they were good at."

She raised an eyebrow. "And?"

"They told me."

She nodded. "That's it, you know. That's the job. Helping them see that they *matter*. That they already have something inside worth building on."

"When a kid believes they're good at something," she continued, "even just one thing, they start to show up differently. Shoulders back. Head up. That's when they engage. That's when they trust. And that's when real learning starts."

Mitchell glanced toward the reset zone. A student had left a sticky note on the wall:

Thanks for helping me believe I'm not dumb.

He swallowed hard.

"You didn't teach that," Tammy said, reading his face. "You uncovered it."

He sat down slowly. "Why don't they tell us this in training?"

Tammy smiled. "Because the best parts of teaching can't be scripted. They have to be *lived*."

She headed for the door, then paused.

"Here's the legacy, Karns. It's not what you taught. It's what you helped them discover about themselves."

As she disappeared down the hall, Mitchell turned back to the board.

EDUCERE.

He underlined it twice.

Then, underneath it, in his own handwriting, he added:

My job isn't to fix what's missing. It's to reveal what's already there.

That afternoon, he added a new note to the student wall:

You're not here to become like everyone else. You're here to become fully you.

And as the last bell echoed through the halls, he looked around Room 211. It didn't look much different. But it felt different. Brighter. More honest. Room 211 wasn't just a classroom anymore.

It was a place where brilliance had been brought to light.

He reached for a marker and wrote above the board:

Find their brilliance and reflect it back to them.

Because real teaching wasn't about raising scores.

It was about raising *sightlines*.

Helping students see their worth, even before they believe it themselves.

CHAPTER

25

THE ONE DEGREE THAT CHANGES EVERYTHING

MITCHELL HADN'T PLANNED on saying yes.

The invitation had come through email: *We'd love for you to speak to our incoming teachers in the alternative certification program. Just a short keynote to share your first-year journey.*

He'd stared at it for a full five minutes before almost deleting it. Keynote? He still felt like he was learning how to take attendance without missing someone.

But something held his hand back from clicking delete.

Tammy had said something to him just last week, after his class ended in chaos that somehow found its way back to calm.

"You don't have to wait until you're a veteran to lead. Sometimes, the most honest voice in the room is the one that just walked through the fire."

That line had stayed with him.

So, he'd said yes.

Now, standing in the back of a multipurpose room filled with plastic chairs, flickering fluorescent lights, and forty anxious new teachers clutching coffee cups and clipboards, Mitchell felt his knees tremble.

He'd been asked to close the session. The keynote speaker. Him.

He glanced down at the notecards in his hands. A few scribbled thoughts. Quotes. A sticky note taped to the last one read: *You've already lived the message. Just tell the truth.*

The facilitator called his name.

He walked to the front, no podium, no slideshow, just a whiteboard and a dry-erase marker. He cleared his throat.

"Hi. I'm Mitchell Karns. I teach seventh-grade math. Room 211."

A few polite nods. A quiet rustle of paper.

"This time last year, I was sitting where you are. Fresh out of training. I had color-coded binders. Perfectly planned slides. I knew the content inside and out."

He paused.

"And none of that saved me."

A soft ripple of nervous laughter.

"What did?" he asked aloud. "That's what I've been trying to figure out."

He turned to the whiteboard and wrote in large letters:

Room 212

"That's what saved me," he said. "Not the room number. The person inside it."

He turned back to the group.

"Her name is Tammy. She taught across the hall. And without even knowing it, she gave me the most powerful professional development I've ever received. Not through handouts. Not through meetings. Through modeling."

Mitchell set the marker down.

He looked out at the group and said simply,

"212. The one-degree shift that changes everything."

Behind him, the first slide appeared on the screen:

The 212° Framework: Ten Transformational Principles of Exceptional Teaching.

He took a breath.

"I didn't invent this," he said. "I lived it. Ten things I saw change a classroom—and a teacher."

He clicked to the next slide.

1. **Lead With Connection** – Connection isn't part of the job. It *is* the job.

2. **Believe Out Loud** – They don't rise to pressure. They rise to your belief.

3. **Presence Over Perfection** – You don't have to be perfect to be great. Just keep showing up.

4. **Teach Beyond the Standard** – We don't just raise scores. We raise humans.

5. **Empower Student Voice** – Students don't just want to feel seen. They need to be heard.

6. **Build Unshakable Resilience** – It's not how many times they fall. It's how many times they *believe* they can rise.

7. **Start With Strengths** – Start with what they're good at. That's how you build who they're becoming.

8. **Anchor in Consistency** – Great classrooms aren't built on rules. They're anchored by consistency.

9. **Celebrate With Joy** – Celebrate effort. Spark joy. Make learning unforgettable.

10. **Draw Out Brilliance** – You're not teaching to their limits. You're teaching to their potential.

He turned back to the room.

"I didn't invent these," he repeated. "I observed them—day after day, across the hall."

His voice dropped slightly.

"I failed constantly this year. I doubted myself. I messed up lessons. I misread situations. But Tammy? She didn't preach. She just showed up. With these."

He tapped the board. "This is what I saw, and what I tried to live. It all comes back to relationships. Students rise when they know you care about them, believe in them, and want what's best for them. That's the foundation. When students trust you, they'll follow you. And that's what teaching really is: not just delivering content, but building belief, one relationship at a time."

He paused, then added, "And if you're wondering whether it works, let me show you what it looks like in real students."

He pointed to the list, moving down it slowly:

1. *Lead With Connection*

   "Jasmine came to class every day hidden behind her hoodie and headphones. I didn't start with a lesson. I started with her name. Now? She helps other students feel seen too."

2. *Believe Out Loud*

   "Marcus pushed every limit. Sarcasm, disruption, defiance. But belief changed everything. I gave him responsibility before he earned it. He rose to meet it."

3. *Presence Over Perfection*

   "I failed more than I succeeded. But I kept showing up. And the students? They started showing up too."

4. *Teach Beyond the Standard*

   "Camila barely spoke. But her drawings spoke volumes. When I finally stopped focusing on the test and asked her what she loved, she gave me a masterpiece."

5. *Empower Student Voice*

"Jada was great at academics but disconnected. Until she helped redesign a lesson for the class. That day, she didn't just lead learning. She led her peers."

6. *Build Unshakable Resilience*

"Johnny never believed he was smart. Until game night. Until the day he stood up and shared his project. Confidence rewired him."

7. *Start With Strengths*

"One girl wrote poems in the margins. A boy coached classmates through hard problems. When I stopped looking for weaknesses, I found their strengths."

8. *Anchor in Consistency*

"We built a reset zone. No punishment. Just routine. Just calm. It didn't fix everything, but it made safety visible."

9. *Celebrate With Joy*

"We laughed. We high-fived wrong answers. We clapped when someone finally asked a question. And students started wanting to come back."

10. *Draw Out Brilliance*

"We didn't fix kids. We uncovered what was already there. One strength. One story. One voice at a time."

He let the silence hang.

"At 211 degrees, I was delivering content. At 212, I started connecting with kids. And that one degree changed everything."

He stepped forward.

"You see at 211 degrees, water is hot. But at 212, it boils. That one extra degree? It makes steam. And steam moves things. It powers engines. It creates movement."

He paused to let that settle.

"So, what does that mean for you?" he continued. "It means your job isn't to be perfect. Or polished. Or Pinterest-ready. It means your job is to find that one degree. Every day. Not to leap up the mountain. Just to step one degree closer than yesterday."

He looked across the room of new faces. He saw his own fear in them. His own hope, too.

"And here's what I want to tell you," he said. "If you're paying attention, you'll find a Tammy in your school. A Room 212. It might not be the number on the door, but you'll feel it. It's the classroom that calms the chaos. The teacher that doesn't flinch when the fire alarm rings. The one who makes kids feel like they matter, even on the days they don't say it out loud."

He paused, then added: "And you know what else? You don't have to just find Room 212. You have the potential to be it. For your students. For your colleagues. For the teacher next door who's barely hanging on."

He pointed to the board again.

"You don't need a title. Or a platform. Or a magic curriculum. You just need the willingness to show up, to be present, consistent, human. And when you do? You're not just teaching. You're transforming."

There was a long silence. No one shifted in their seats.

Mitchell took a slow breath and smiled.

"Teaching isn't about control. It's about connection. And your job isn't to fix kids. It's to remind them they were never broken, just becoming."

He picked up the marker one last time and wrote beneath the list: *One degree. That's all it takes.*

He let the marker drop into the tray.

"One degree," he repeated, turning back to the room. "You want to know how to live that?"

He pointed, then started moving down the list again:

"It's greeting a student by name when they expect to be ignored.

"It's pausing before you react and choosing patience instead of power.

"It's asking what's going on before asking where the homework is.

"It's noticing the kid who never raises their hand and inviting their voice anyway.

"It's not the perfect lesson plan. It's the second chance. The clean slate. The quiet reminder that someone still believes in them.

"It's realizing that rigor doesn't come before relationship. It grows from it.

"It's writing one kid a sticky note that says, 'I see your effort.'

"It's saying, 'I'm glad you're here,' even when they show up late."

He looked across the room again.

"These aren't grand gestures. They're not flashy. They don't go viral. But they build trust. They build belief. They build kids."

He nodded toward the board one final time.

"That's the one degree. And you carry it with you every time you choose people over performance."

He stepped back from the board, the room still silent.

No applause. No music. Just forty new teachers sitting a little straighter—like maybe they believed they could do this.

Mitchell let the moment breathe.

"You don't have to be Tammy," he said quietly. "But you do have to show up. And when you do, even one degree more than yesterday, you become the difference."

He glanced once more at the words on the board. Then turned, nodded, and walked off.

Not because he had it all figured out.

But because he had given them what they needed most: permission to believe they could be the one degree.

Later that evening, he sat in his car outside the school where the professional development had been held. The sun was just beginning to dip below the horizon, casting gold across the dashboard.

He pulled his journal from the passenger seat and flipped to a blank page.

At the top, he wrote:

Tammy wasn't just across the hall. She was my daily professional development.

Then:

Room 212 wasn't a classroom. It was a masterclass.

A masterclass in what matters most.

And these ten principles?

They weren't created in a binder. They were modeled in real time by one teacher, one room, one degree at a time.

Now they belonged to him.

He paused, then added one last line:

If you lead with connection, believe out loud, and stay faithful, you'll become the teacher every student needs, and the leader every school deserves.

He closed the journal, placed it in the glove box, and exhaled.

It's not the curriculum.

It's not technology.

The teacher is the difference maker.

Always has been. Always will be.

CHAPTER
26

WHAT THEY REMEMBER

THE FINAL BELL had rung.

Students poured out of the building like they always did, backpacks bouncing, laughter echoing, summer in their eyes. But inside Room 211, Mitchell Karns sat motionless.

The room was quiet now. Far quieter than usual. But not a quiet of absence. One of meaning. Contentment.

Desks slightly crooked. A few pencils scattered on the floor. One backpack left behind, already claimed by the lost and found. On the whiteboard, a quote still hung:

They may not remember the lessons. But they'll remember they mattered.

Mitchell reached into the top drawer and pulled out a worn sticky note, the one he had scribbled in desperation during his second week, when he felt like quitting wasn't just an option, but an inevitability.

Grace before grades. Patience before programs. Love before lessons.

He stared at the handwriting for a long time. It had been a lifeline then. Now it was a mirror. A reflection of everything that had become true.

He had grown.

And the most beautiful part?

So had they.

Jasmine, once guarded, had started raising her hand, offering her voice without apology.

Marcus, the class comedian turned class leader, had gone from defiant to dependable.

Johnny, invisible on day one, had become indispensable.

Camila, silent for months, had been seen. And had begun to speak, not just in words, but in sketches, in moments, in kind acts.

The entire class had learned that learning is stronger when it's shared—and that the best ideas often come from working together.

None of it came from a perfect lesson. Not one breakthrough could be traced to a worksheet or warm-up.

It came from patience. From seeing. From showing up.

It came from Room 212.

He smiled, remembering his first morning, the binder, the pacing guide, the carefully prepared plan that unraveled by third period. He'd felt like he was drowning. And now?

Still tired. But not drowning.

There was a single knock at the open door.

Camila.

She stepped inside quietly, both hands holding a folded piece of notebook paper. Her backpack was already slung over one shoulder.

"I made this," she said softly, offering it like it was something fragile.

Mitchell unfolded it slowly.

It was a sketch of their classroom, figures at desks, with details only a student could know: the crack in the tile by the front row, the corner shelf where the tissue box always tilted, the reset zone mat in the back. On the whiteboard in the sketch, a message:

You Matter.

At the bottom, in careful pencil:

Thank you for seeing me.

He blinked hard.

When he looked up, she was already turning to leave.

"Camila," he started, but didn't finish the sentence.

She paused, smiled shyly, and disappeared down the hall.

No big goodbye.

Just a moment.

The kind that stays.

He stayed in his seat for a while, the drawing trembling slightly in his hands.

As the sun lowered and the building settled into its summer hush, Tammy appeared in the doorway, a coffee in hand.

"Still here?" she asked.

He held up the note.

She stepped forward, leaned in to read it, and nodded.

"She gets it," she said softly.

Mitchell glanced around the room. The walls, now bare, held no charts or student work. But somehow, it didn't feel empty.

It felt full.

Not with posters or papers—but with presence. With the memory of voices that had been heard, strengths that had been seen, and hearts that had begun to believe.

A space that had held chaos and calm. Laughter and tears. Mistakes. Second chances. Breakthroughs.

"They won't remember everything I taught them," he said.

"No," Tammy replied. "But they'll remember how you made them feel. That you believed in them. That you showed up every day."

She touched the corner of the sketch, then looked up.

"Most won't tell you. Not now. Maybe not ever. But this?" She gestured to the paper. "This means they know."

Mitchell nodded slowly.

"You want to be the teacher they remember?" she added. "Don't aim for the spotlight. Aim for the heart. It's quieter, but it lasts a lifetime."

He stood and walked to the whiteboard. Beneath the quote already written, he picked up the marker one last time and added:

They may not remember the lessons. But they'll remember you cared.

Tammy gave the words a long look.

"You've figured it out," she said.

Mitchell smiled. "I had help."

She raised an eyebrow. "Barely."

He let out a quiet laugh, then paused.

"But honestly, in case I haven't said it… Thank you. For everything. I wouldn't have survived this year without you."

Tammy tilted her head, smiling warmly. "It's what we do. We show up. For the kids. For each other."

Then with a playful smirk: "So… See you at preplanning in August, Karns?"

He nodded, smile deepening. "Wouldn't miss it."

She gave him a mock salute, knocked twice on the doorframe (her signature) one final time. and vanished down the hallway.

Mitchell watched her go, then turned and sat down.

He thought about everything she had taught him, not through speeches or strategies, but through her consistency. Her calm. Her belief.

Room 212 had never just been a room.

It had been a compass.

A model.

A quiet revolution.

He looked out the window. The sun was low now, casting golden light across the desks, casting soft shadows on the floor. The kind of light that turns ordinary moments into lasting memories.

He opened his journal to the last page.

Year One:

- *I failed. Often.*
- *I doubted. Constantly.*
- *I kept showing up. Always.*

Then he wrote one more line:

It's important to know my subject, but it's even more important to know my students.

He stood to gather his things, but paused.

There, written at the top of the whiteboard in a familiar hand:

One meaningful relationship can change the trajectory of a life.

He smiled.

Of course it was her. One final lesson. One perfect reminder of why this work matters.

He stepped back and read it again.

Then, with the last bit of sunlight casting soft gold across Room 211, Mitchell smiled, whispering.

"Amen."

And turned off the lights.

About the Author

Dr. Brad Johnson is a former teacher and administrator turned internationally recognized speaker and bestselling author. Ranked the **#3 Global Guru in Education** and named a **Top 100 Influencer in Education by District Administration (2025)**, he's spent over thirty years helping educators rediscover their **passion, power, and purpose**.

Brad is the author of more than fifteen books, including *Empowering Students*, *Relational Intelligence*, *Becoming a More Assertive Teacher*, and the bestselling *Dear Teacher*. His work centers on **relational and transformational leadership**—equipping educators to lead with connection, build trust, and create schools where people matter more than policies.

He has keynoted for tens of thousands of educators across **twelve countries** and hosts the podcast *Lattes with Leaders*. But at heart, Brad's still a teacher—grateful for the ones who showed him what real impact looks like.

Room 212 is a tribute to them—the steady, compassionate educators who don't chase the spotlight but leave a legacy anyway.

To learn more, book a keynote, or access free resources, visit:

Room212Book.com

DoctorBradJohnson.com

You've Read the Story. Now Live the Shift.

Room 212 isn't just a story. It's a model. A mindset. A movement.

The following study guide takes the heart of the book and turns it into real-world strategies for teachers, teams, and schools.

Whether you're reading solo or leading a PD session, this guide will help you turn inspiration into action—one degree at a time.

Let's begin.

A Relational Teaching Framework for Educators Who Believe in Connection Over Compliance

Overview

This guide accompanies the teacher fable *Room 212* and transforms story into strategy. It's built for classroom educators, mentors, and school teams ready to move beyond content delivery—and lead through trust, presence, and human connection.

The 212° Framework: Ten Transformational Principles of Exceptional Teaching

The *212° Framework* centers around ten core principles of relational teaching, grouped into three foundational categories:

The Heart of Teaching

The foundation of a classroom where students feel safe, valued, and seen.

1. **Lead with Connection**: Relationships come first. Trust and rapport are the gateway to learning.
2. **Celebrate with Joy**: Recognize effort, progress, and small wins. Joy fuels momentum.

3. **Anchor in Consistency**: Routines create safety. Predictability builds calm and trust.

4. **Start with Strengths**: See and build from what students do well. Confidence creates readiness.

The Mindset Shift

The internal rewiring of what it means to teach with presence and purpose.

5. **Presence Over Perfection**: What students need isn't polish—it's presence. Show up and stay steady.

6. **Believe Out Loud**: Don't just believe in them—say it. Show students what you see in them.

7. **Build Unshakable Resilience**: Model bounce-back. Turn setbacks into strength.

The Impact Multiplier

The practices that expand connection into empowerment and transformation.

8. **Teach Beyond the Standard**: Go beyond curriculum. Teach life. Teach the human behind the data.

9. **Empower Student Voice**: Invite ownership. Let students lead, question, and express.

10. **Draw Out Brilliance**: Every student has genius. Your job is to help them see it.

These principles are more than strategies. They represent a shift in presence, purpose, and practice—transforming classrooms from places of compliance into spaces of possibility where connection leads and empowerment follows.

What You'll Find in Each Chapter

Each chapter is designed to reflect a key principle and includes:

- **A Core Theme** from the 212º Framework
- **A Power Quote** to anchor the message
- **A Teaching Insight** that distills the chapter's key idea
- **A Classroom Lens** with real-world application strategies
- **Reflection Questions** to guide solo or group discussion
- **A Try This** prompt for immediate action
- **A PD Strategy** for coaching, facilitation, or team growth

How to Use This Study Guide

Room 212 isn't just a story—it's a teaching roadmap built for reflection, growth, and classroom transformation.

This guide helps you take the story off the page and into your classroom by aligning each chapter with one of The 212º Framework: Ten Transformational Principles of Exceptional Teaching —a signature framework rooted in belief, safety, and relational presence.

The following list suggests some uses for this guide.

- Solo reflection

  - Read one chapter per week and journal your responses.
  - Choose a Try This strategy to test out each week.
  - Use the 212° Framework to guide your teaching philosophy.

- Team book study

  - Meet weekly to discuss one or two chapters at a time.
  - Rotate facilitation using the Reflection Questions and PD Strategies.

- Use the Themes to reflect on student engagement, burnout, and classroom culture.

- Mentoring and coaching

  - Use the Classroom Lens to support early-career teachers.

  - Reflect on each chapter during observation follow-ups or mentoring sessions.

  - Explore how relational teaching reshapes classroom outcomes.

- Workshops and PD days

  - Build breakout sessions around the 10 Principles

  - Use the Power Quotes, Try This prompts, and Reflection Questions to guide sessions.

  - End each session by asking: "What's your one-degree shift?"

The power of this guide is in the conversation it creates—with yourself, your students, and your team. Use it with intention. Revisit it often.

Because great teaching isn't about perfection.

It's about presence.

Chapter 1—The Second Career

Theme: Presence Over Perfection

Power Quote: "You don't have to be perfect to be great—just consistent for them."

Teaching Insight: Mitchell's leap into teaching shows that the most powerful educators aren't the most polished—they're the most present. Students don't need superheroes. They need steady ones.

Classroom Lens:
- You don't have to feel ready to be impactful.
- Presence often matters more than experience.

Reflection Questions:
- Where in your work are you feeling uncertain—but called?
- How do you define meaning in the work?
- What moment made you realize teaching was your real calling?

Try This: Write down the moment that made you become a teacher. Post it where you can see it each morning.

PD Strategy: Open your meeting with the question: "When did you know you were meant to teach?" Share aloud.

Chapter 2—Welcome to Room 211

Theme: Teach Beyond the Standard

Power Quote: "We don't just raise scores—we raise humans."

Teaching Insight: Mitchell's first full day reminds us that students don't remember lessons—they remember how they were treated. Teaching beyond the standard means seeing beyond the surface.

Classroom Lens:
- Show students they matter more than their data.
- Teach the student first, then the standard.

Reflection Questions:
- What does it mean to teach beyond the standard?
- What would your teaching look like if humanity led your instruction?
- How do you show students they matter outside of academics?

Try This: Begin one lesson this week with a connection—not a standard.

PD Strategy: Ask: How do we define success beyond test scores? Brainstorm alternative measures together.

Chapter 3—Not in the Brochure

Theme: Build Unshakable Resilience

Power Quote: "The strongest classrooms are led by teachers who refused to quit on the hard days."

Teaching Insight: Chaos, doubt, and tough moments aren't failures—they're the real job. Resilient classrooms are built by resilient teachers who respond with calm, care, and conviction.

Classroom Lens:
- Respond to chaos with calm.
- Model bounce-back behavior for your students.

Reflection Questions:
- What's one moment that almost made you quit?
- How do you model resilience when the day goes sideways?
- Where do your students need to see bounce-back modeled this week?

Try This: Share one personal story of struggle and growth with your class.

PD Strategy: What does resilience look like in our school culture? Share examples of bounce-back moments from the year.

Chapter 4—The Teacher Across the Hall

Theme: Lead With Connection

Power Quote: "Connection isn't part of the job—it is the job."

Teaching Insight: Tammy's presence at the door isn't a routine—it's a philosophy. She teaches Mitchell (and us) that connection always precedes compliance, correction, and curriculum.

Classroom Lens:
- Greet students with intentionality.
- Use names, eye contact, and curiosity as connection tools.

Reflection Questions:
- What routines do you have to build connection before instruction?
- Who is one student you need to reconnect with this week?
- How does your presence shape student trust?

Try This: Greet every student tomorrow by name—with eye contact and a genuine question.

PD Strategy: Role-play connection-first greetings with a partner. Debrief how it felt on both sides.

Chapter 5—The Observation

Theme: Anchor in Consistency

Power Quote: "Great classrooms aren't built on rules—they're anchored by consistency."

Teaching Insight: Mitchell learns that strong culture doesn't require control—it requires rhythm. Routines create safety. Predictability creates permission to engage.

Classroom Lens:
- • Routines calm the room.
- • Predictability builds trust.

Reflection Questions:
- • What's one routine that anchors your classroom culture?
- • Where might inconsistency be causing confusion or stress?
- • How can you make your expectations more visible and consistent?

Try This: Choose one routine to tighten this week. Practice it with intention.

PD Strategy: What routines define our school culture—and where do we need more consistency?

Chapter 6—Why Are You Really Here?

Theme: Empower Student Voice

Power Quote: "Some students need us to believe in them until them believe in themselves."

Teaching Insight: This chapter reframes purpose—not as a job description, but as a mission rooted in presence and listening. It's not about why you teach content, but why you're showing up for kids.

Classroom Lens:

- Ask questions that invite student voice.
- Remember: presence before planning.

Reflection Questions:

- When was the last time a student surprised you with their insight?
- How does your classroom amplify or silence student voice?
- Why are you *really* here—and how does that show in your teaching?

Try This: Ask students what they need more of from you—then try one thing they suggest.

PD Strategy: What's the difference between teaching content and teaching humans? Discuss as a group.

Chapter 7—You Don't Teach Content. You Teach Humans.

Theme: Start With Strengths

Power Quote: "Start with their strengths—that's where confidence begins."

Teaching Insight: The most successful lessons don't just hit standards—they honor the students behind the data. Great teachers look beyond performance to possibility.

Classroom Lens:
- Use strengths as the entry point to challenge.
- Start with what students do well, not what they lack.

Reflection Questions:
- How do you discover and build on your students' strengths?
- What strengths have you overlooked in your quietest learners?
- What would your lessons look like if you planned from strength first?

Try This: Give one student a leadership role based on a nonacademic strength you've observed.

PD Strategy: What are three strengths your class brings that don't show up in test scores? Have each group member share.

Chapter 8—The Problem Isn't the Kids

Theme: Consistency Starts With Us

Power Quote: "Before we blame the student, we have to check the system and ourselves."

Teaching Insight: Before we correct behavior, we must correct inconsistency. Mitchell learns that behavior isn't just a student issue—it's often a reflection of leadership. Students don't need more rules. They need more clarity, connection, and consistent presence.

Classroom Lens:

- Ask: *"Is it the kid—or the inconsistency?"*
- Calm is built through rhythm, not reaction.
- The mirror matters—students reflect what we model.

Reflection Questions:

- Where does inconsistency show up in your classroom or school?
- What systems support predictability for students?
- How can you lead with steadiness, even in moments of chaos?

Try This: Audit one classroom routine that feels "off" and refine it with clarity and consistency.

PD Strategy: Invite staff to share: *Describe a time when student behavior mirrored adult inconsistency—and what you learned from it.*

Chapter 9—Control Versus Connection

Theme: Build Unshakable Resilience

Power Quote: "It's not how many times they fall—it's how many times they believe they can rise."

Teaching Insight: This chapter reminds us that control is an illusion—but connection builds resilience. A trusted teacher doesn't just manage behavior—they empower students to own it.

Classroom Lens:
- Teach emotional regulation before academic rigor.
- Connection calms the nervous system. Lead from that space.

Reflection Questions:
- When have you chosen connection over control?
- What tools help students bounce back in your class?
- What's one area where you could release control for greater trust?

Try This: Name one struggle a student faced this week—and affirm their resilience out loud.

PD Strategy: Share one story where connection, not control, changed a situation.

Chapter 10—Relationships Before Rigor

Theme: Teach Beyond the Standard

Power Quote: "You can't teach their minds until you reach their hearts."

Teaching Insight: Content matters—but connection unlocks it. This chapter flips the script; before rigor can thrive, relationships must lead. Because if they don't feel safe, they can't learn.

Classroom Lens:

- Greet first. Correct second.
- Teach the person, not the plan.

Reflection Questions:

- What does it mean to prioritize relationships before rigor?
- How does trust show up in your classroom routines?
- Where can you slow down rigor to speed up relationships?

Try This: Begin class with a nonacademic check-in before diving into instruction.

PD Strategy: How do we balance high expectations with high trust? Ask your team.

Chapter 11—The Table in the Corner

Theme: Lead With Connection

Power Quote: "Connection isn't part of the job—it is the job."

Teaching Insight: A teacher's lunchroom table becomes a metaphor for inclusion. This chapter shows that connection doesn't happen by accident—it's built intentionally, especially with those who feel left out.

Classroom Lens:

- Look for the "corner table" students—those emotionally isolated.

Strong relationships don't grow in the crowd—they're forged in the quiet moments with individuals and small groups.

Reflection Questions:

- Who is your "corner table" this week?
- What systems unintentionally exclude students in your room?
- How can you invite someone back into community?

Try This: Sit with a student or colleague you usually don't. Ask them something real.

PD Strategy: Who's sitting in the emotional corner of our building—and how do we draw them in? Discuss as a team.

Chapter 12—Seeing the Students

Theme: Empower Student Voice

Power Quote: "They need to be seen, known, and heard—especially when they go quiet."

Teaching Insight: The kids who fly under the radar are often those who most need your attention. Voice isn't always loud. Sometimes, it's silent—but present.

Classroom Lens:

- Value the introverts. Hear the ones who whisper.
- Eye contact and nonverbals often speak louder than participation.

Reflection Questions:

- Which students haven't spoken much this week?
- How do you affirm quiet strengths in your class?
- How can you show a student they matter without words?

Try This: Notice one student's nonverbal cues. Acknowledge their presence intentionally.

PD Strategy: Reflect on the difference between compliant and connected students.

Chapter 13—Reach Them Where They Live

Theme: Believe Out Loud

Power Quote: "Let them borrow your belief until they find their own."

Teaching Insight: You can't inspire from a distance. This chapter shows that when you step into a student's world—literally or emotionally—you earn the right to influence it.

Classroom Lens:

- Belief isn't generic. It's specific.
- Don't just believe in students—show them what you believe about them.

Reflection Questions:

- What's one belief your students need to hear from you?
- How do you show up in their world, not just your classroom?
- What's one way you can personalize your encouragement?

Try This: Tell one student exactly what you see in them. Be specific and sincere.

PD Strategy: What do you want your students to believe about themselves by year's end? Have each group member share.

Chapter 14—Love Who You Teach

Theme: Build Unshakable Resilience

Power Quote: "Love what you teach, but love who you teach more!"

Teaching Insight: Love is not soft. It's the strongest force you can bring into a classroom. And it shows up most when students are at their worst.

Classroom Lens:
- Love = boundaries + belief.
- Every correction is a chance to say, "I'm still here."

Reflection Questions:
- What does love look like in your classroom management?
- How do you express care when correcting behavior?
- Which student needs tough love rooted in belief this week?

Try This: Say, "I care too much about you to let that slide"—and mean it.

PD Strategy: When did love—not consequence—change your mindset or behavior? Discuss as a team.

Chapter 15—Camila Doesn't Talk

Theme: Lead With Connection

Power Quote: "Some students speak in silence. Be the teacher who hears them too."

Teaching Insight: Camila teaches us that presence speaks volumes. When words aren't there, behavior and creativity become the language. Connection means learning how each child communicates trust.

Classroom Lens:

- Drawings, posture, eye contact—learn their language.
- Quiet students are not disengaged—they're deliberate.

Reflection Questions:

- Who is your Camila this year?
- What alternative forms of communication do your students use?
- How can you validate student expression beyond participation?

Try This: Compliment a student's nonverbal contribution today (art, support, kindness, expression).

PD Strategy: Share silent ways your students express trust. What would you miss if you weren't looking?

Chapter 16—Give Me a Break

Theme: Presence Over Perfection

Power Quote: "You don't have to be perfect to be great—just consistent for them."

Teaching Insight: This chapter is a reality check—teachers aren't superheroes. Breaks aren't luxuries—they're leadership strategies. Presence can't be sustained without boundaries.

Classroom Lens:

- Model balance. If you're depleted, you're not present.
- Boundaries build longevity.

Reflection Questions:

- Where do you give too much without recharging?
- How can you model healthy limits for students?
- What's one way to protect your presence this week?

Try This: Take a five-minute presence reset between classes. Breathe. Reflect. Then re-engage.

PD Strategy: Open with this prompt—What does "rest as resistance" mean in your role?

Chapter 17—Embracing Setbacks

Theme: Start With Strengths

Power Quote: "If students never experience success, why would they believe success is possible?"

Teaching Insight: Students don't need to avoid failure—they need to learn how to rise from it. This chapter shows how teachers can turn setbacks into strength-finding moments.

Classroom Lens:
- Strengths don't mean perfection. They mean growth pathways.
- Normalize struggle. Celebrate bounce-backs.

Reflection Questions:
- How do you frame failure in your classroom?
- What language do you use when students fall short?
- Which student needs help reframing a recent mistake?

Try This: Catch a student succeeding after a setback. Point it out publicly or privately.

PD Strategy: Share one "bounce-back" story from your class. What made the turnaround happen?

Chapter 18—The Power of Yet

Theme: Celebrate With Joy

Power Quote: "Celebrate effort. Spark joy. Make learning unforgettable."

Teaching Insight: *Yet* is one of the most powerful words in education. This chapter reminds us that student hope hinges on your reaction to struggle—and your commitment to celebration.

Classroom Lens:

- Joy builds momentum.
- Celebrate effort as often as achievement.

Reflection Questions:

- How do you react when students say, "I can't"?
- What's the last thing you celebrated in class?
- How can joy become a ritual in your room?

Try This: Create a "Yet Wall" where students add things they're learning—but have not mastered.

PD Strategy: What do you celebrate besides grades? Have each group member share.

Chapter 19—Step-Up Night

Theme: Teach Beyond the Standard

Power Quote: "Sometimes all it takes is one teacher to believe—and it becomes the beginning of everything."

Teaching Insight: Parent Night isn't just about presenting—it's about partnering. This chapter reframes how we build trust with families by showing them we see more than data.

Classroom Lens:
- Parents need to know their child is seen, known, and believed in.
- Standards matter—but so does humanity.

Reflection Questions:
- How do you connect with families beyond academics?
- What does it mean to teach the whole child?
- What message do parents get from your communication style?

Try This: Send one positive message home this week to a family—no matter how small the win.

PD Strategy: Ask your team—What's one way to rehumanize our communication with families?

Chapter 20—Data Informs. Relationships Transform.

Theme: Presence Over Perfection

Power Quote: "Data can tell you what—they can tell you *why*."

Teaching Insight: This chapter is a mic drop. It's not about ignoring data—it's about decoding it through relationships. The most powerful insights don't come from spreadsheets. They come from knowing your kids.

Classroom Lens:
- Use data as a signal—not a verdict.
- Look beyond the numbers. Listen to the stories.

Reflection Questions:
- How do relationships shape the way you interpret data?
- Where has a student outperformed their data because of connection?
- How can we train ourselves to see *behind* the numbers?

Try This: Choose one student and talk to them about their learning—not their grades.

PD Strategy: When have you seen relationships transform what data alone couldn't? Discuss as a team.

Chapter 21—Fire Drill Wisdom

Theme: Lead With Connection

Power Quote: "Add to the calm, not the chaos."

Teaching Insight: Moments of disruption reveal the depth of trust. This chapter reminds us that connection isn't built in chaos—but it's revealed by it. In a crisis, students don't look for a policy—they look for a person.

Classroom Lens:

- The calmest voice leads the room.
- When in doubt, be the adult they can count on.

Reflection Questions:

- What small disruptions test your classroom's emotional safety?
- How do your students respond to your presence in chaos?
- What habits help you stay grounded under pressure?

Try This: Choose one stressful moment this week and respond 10 percent slower, 10 percent calmer.

PD Strategy: What was your last "fire drill" moment? What did it reveal about your culture? Have each team member share.

Chapter 22—You Don't Need a Title to Lead

Theme: Empower Student Voice

Power Quote: "Leadership isn't a role. It's a ripple effect."

Teaching Insight: This chapter shifts the narrative. Leadership isn't for a few students—it's a skill all students can practice. Your job? Make room for it.

Classroom Lens:

- Empower students to lead in their lane.
- Invite leadership before they ask for it.

Reflection Questions:

- Who are the hidden leaders in your classroom?
- How do you make space for student voice in daily routines?
- What's one leadership task you can delegate this week?

Try This: Assign a rotating "culture leader" role to affirm kindness, support peers, and guide tone.

PD Strategy: How do we redefine student leadership to include more than the usual suspects? Discuss as a group.

Chapter 23—The Power of Small Wins

Theme: Believe Out Loud

Power Quote: "Celebrate the little victories—because they're what build belief."

Teaching Insight: This chapter reminds us that momentum is made of moments. The teacher who sees the first step, not just the finish line, builds unstoppable confidence.

Classroom Lens:
- Every student needs to feel progress.
- Catch them winning, even if the win is tiny.

Reflection Questions:
- What's one small win you overlooked this week?
- How do you show students you notice their growth?
- How do small wins change your energy as a teacher?

Try This: End one lesson this week with a thirty-second win share. Let students name what they did well.

PD Strategy: What is one overlooked win from this month? Share it aloud.

Chapter 24—Help Them Find Their Brilliance

Theme: Draw Out Brilliance

Power Quote: "You're not teaching to their limits—you're teaching to their potential."

Teaching Insight: This is the soul of Room 212. You're not just filling gaps—you're helping kids discover who they are. It's not remediation. It's revelation.

Classroom Lens:
- Ask, "What makes this student light up?"
- Name the brilliance before they believe it.

Reflection Questions:
- What does it mean to teach to potential—not performance?
- What strengths have your students shown outside the curriculum?
- Which student needs help discovering their brilliance this week?

Try This: Write a note to one student naming a strength they may not see yet.

PD Strategy: Who was the first person to call out your brilliance? Reflect and share.

Chapter 25—The One Degree That Changes Everything

Theme: The 212º Framework Overview

Power Quote: "At 211 degrees, water is hot. At 212 degrees, it boils. That one extra degree makes all the difference."

Teaching Insight: This chapter ties it all together. The greatest transformations are rooted in small, intentional shifts. The one-degree mindset isn't about doing more—it's about doing what matters.

Classroom Lens:

- Focus on one degree, not 100-percent change.
- Small acts of connection yield massive momentum.

Reflection Questions:

- What's your one-degree shift this year?
- Which principle from the 212º Framework resonates most— and why?
- How will you lead with presence going forward?

Try This: Post your one-degree goal on your desk, mirror, or planner. Revisit it daily.

PD Strategy: Ask each staff member to name their one-degree action for the next month.

Chapter 26—What They Remember

Theme: Final Reflection

Power Quote: "Students won't remember every lesson—but they'll never forget how you made them feel."

Teaching Insight: This final chapter reminds us that legacy isn't measured by your syllabus. It's measured by presence. The teacher in Room 212 didn't aim for perfection. She aimed for impact—and she got there, one degree at a time.

Classroom Lens:

- Every moment is a memory in the making.
- They remember your tone, your eyes, your belief—long after your lessons.

Reflection Questions:

- What do you want students to remember most about being in your room?
- What one word would they use to describe your impact?
- What do you want your teaching legacy to be?

Try This: Write your own teacher legacy statement. Keep it where you can see it. Live it daily.

PD Strategy: Close your PD session with a circle. Ask each person to share what they want students to remember about them.

Bringing It All Together: The Real Work Starts Here

Room 212 is more than a book. It's a mirror, a challenge, and a conversation starter.

Every chapter is a reminder: Teaching isn't just what you deliver—it's what you inspire in others.

You've now walked through 26 chapters of presence, connection, belief, and small, intentional shifts. But insight alone isn't transformation.

Now it's your turn.

This guide isn't meant to sit on a shelf. It's built for:

- **Team Retreats** — Break the chapters into sessions and let each teacher lead one.
- **Coaching Conversations** — Use the reflection questions to get beneath the surface.
- **Staff Development** — Start each staff meeting with one chapter's Power Quote or Try This.
- **Book Study Series** — Run a ten-week PD around The 212° Framework: Ten Transformational Principles of Exceptional Teaching No matter how you use it—do one thing:

Teach where you are. Not with perfection. Not with power. But with presence.

Because the most impactful teachers aren't the ones who do it all. They're the ones who make one-degree shifts that change everything.

So show up. Believe out loud. Lead with connection.

And remember:

"You'll get there. Just don't let the noise make you forget why you're here."

That's what the teacher in Room 212 did. Now it's your turn.